THE CHILD

THE CHILD

Pascale Kramer

Translated by Tamsin Black

Bellevue Literary Press
New York

First Published in the United States in 2013 by
Bellevue Literary Press, New York

FOR INFORMATION CONTACT:
Bellevue Literary Press
NYU School of Medicine
550 First Avenue
OBV A612
New York, NY 10016

Library of Congress Cataloging-in-Publication Data
Kramer, Pascale, 1961–
[Un homme ébranlé. English]
The child/by Pascale Kramer; translated by Tamsin Black.—1st ed.
p. cm.
ISBN 978-1-934137-55-0 (pbk.)
I. Black, Tamsin. II. Title.
PQ2671.R287H6613 2012
843'.914—dc23
2012032068

Bellevue Literary Press would like to thank all its generous donors—individuals and foundations—for their support.

This publication is made possible by the New York State Council on the Arts with the support of Governor Andrew Cuomo and the New York State Legislature

swiss arts council
prohelvetia

and with the support of the Swiss Arts Council Pro Helvetia

Book design and composition by Mulberry Tree Press, Inc.
Manufactured in the United States of America.

FIRST EDITION

1 3 5 7 9 8 6 4 2

ISBN 978-1-934137-55-0

For Fanny,
for Charlotte,
for my nephew Edouard,
for Christophe,
for their childhood.

THE CHILD

SIMONE REALIZED that it was at that same time of year, with the forsythia in bloom, that Claude had first brought her here, to his house in T. The bush was not yet so high that it took up the whole window, but already blackbirds had built a nest among the yellow blooms screening the neighbors' rough-cast wall. The male was there, clinging to the fence, eyeing her through the gaps in the mesh. Simone could see it jerking its head toward her. She had made a move to close the window but froze at the sound of the bell for fear of missing the child's voice. But it was still only Jovana, the mother, answering Claude's terse sentences. They were in the hall, right behind the study door, and Simone stood with her back to it, as though it was not enough to have shut it to show her obedience to the privacy demanded. Jovana might have changed her mind, in which case this plan, which had been so long coming to fruition, then rushed into, in a kind of salutary terror, would have been nothing but pointless torment for everyone. And Claude would have nothing left to salvage before the unimaginable idea of approaching death. Simone hardly dared think that this was what they should hope.

The blackbird had begun to claw at the fence in anxious anticipation of taking flight. Then it would vanish into the top of the plum trees across the lawn beside the long remote box of balconies and ocher tiles, which Simone had always known to be there but which it still pained Claude to think he had allowed to be built. Like a wall of cages, the block loomed out over the white-and-yellow expanse of the garden, causing her, too, a pang of bitterness on this particular day—this relentless day, she could not help thinking

The sliding door of a minivan clanged shut in the silence behind the house; then the blackbird was gone and Simone at last heard the child's clear voice answering Claude. The surprise sent a shudder through her, as though a hand had just yanked at her insides. There, it was done: there could be no turning back. She moved forward to shut the window in the confusion of sudden panic. She could not rid herself of the thought that all this was selfish, selfish and terribly desperate.

She had imagined a boy on the verge of adolescence, but he was still a child, with a thick mop of auburn hair lopped off summarily above the nape of the neck. He was small for his eleven years and his stomach ducked in abruptly, so that his plump little ribs stuck out. The resemblance to Claude was comical in the soft young flesh. Simone wondered if they, too, could see it.

So, this is Gaël. We've already gotten to know each other a bit, Claude observed stiffly. The child squirmed slightly, then stepped forward, as though to see where the light was coming from on the somber wood and leather furniture of the study, where the only signs of life were a row of books and a steel mug with pens sticking out of it. His lips were sucked in, in a kind of expression of sympathy, creating long dimples in his round red cheeks. Simone introduced herself and tried to smile, unsure whether she should kiss a child of his age. He's a brave kid, she caught herself thinking, seeing him hold in his breath and his stomach, his arms thrust like posts deep into his pants pockets. There was something arrestingly sweet and grown-up about his shy eleven-year-old gallantry. Simone could not believe how completely determined he was to be here.

Claude had insisted the visit last at least a few hours, with no thought for how awkward it would be. Gaël had gone over to the trophies and wanted to know who had won them; then he backed away and blushed inexplicably. Claude asked him if he wanted to have a look around, see the photos. The question did not call for an answer, just the assent of them both. His left arm swung beside his body with the twitch that had become almost constant, to disperse or dispel the pain. His eyes sought her out, anxious at what was afoot and that, with the guilt, was having an impact he had not foreseen. Simone raised her eyebrows and stared back with an air of finality, surprise, and annoyance. For he need not think there was anything she could do to counter the crazy decision he had made without her but with so much pointless deliberation. Gaël now knew that his father was not the man he had always thought, but this sports coach with a broad, bony face, his features drawn by the cancer that masked the once probably trusting man who had conceived him and the troubled man she had met not long after. She had been thirty-five at the time. That was ten years ago now. Ten years of a happiness that had been genuine for having been willed, agreed—ten years for nothing, she had thought, to her shame but also her salvation, when the diagnosis was announced.

If Claude died, she had thought, too, it would no longer be she who had been the last person to matter, but this son born of an illicit love that had never fully healed, while she had quite simply never been able to bear it. Jealousy had placed her pain and revolt on hold. Being beside the point suddenly relieved her of the weight of resentment, and sorrow rose to her face. Claude had already disappeared along the corridor, but Gaël saw her eyes cloud with tears and seemed not to know how to turn away from this adult emotion. I never thought you and I would meet, she said to him a little too loudly, embarrassing him for no reason.

It had quickly gotten tempting to suggest going for a drive, so they would not have to look at one another and to pass the time. Claude insisted on taking the wheel, although the pain was shooting down to his fingers—a kind of throbbing, he said, that pulsed right into his bones from his shoulder blades. Gaël spread his arms and grasped the back of the two seats in front, as though to get a better view. Simone was aware of his face close to hers, of his sugary breath and the soft squelch of his teeth pulling on a sticky toffee. They had left the leafy neighborhood with gardens all identically sunny and blossoming hedges that rose halfway up the dingy white of the houses. Claude wanted to show the child the sports ground and the stream that now flowed straight between the concrete banks of the estate. Simone had never known him to fill the silence like this. His peremptory manner and the constant exercises of his left hand, restless with pain, were making her tense. Let's just look for a bit, she suggested as gently as she could. But Claude wanted Gaël to see how the suburb was sprouting dirty big buildings that were being flung up one after another with less and less space between them, just these patches of grass, and where no effort or respect mattered anymore. Rancor had set in well before the sickness, or perhaps with the despondency that had preceded it, and he took a perverse pleasure in it, because he was going to take early leave of a nonsensical era from which he had somehow divorced.

You're boring him, Simone said, trying to joke, frustrated by her inability to alleviate the excruciating torture of these moments. There was a moist crunch of candy, then a cheerful voice as Gaël assured her that, no, Claude was not boring him. He seemed to hesitate about which of the two to oppose. He was resting his strangely full and unmoving face on his chin in the worn fabric of the seat back. Simone noticed that he was looking at Claude—not at the father, but at the sick man—and that he was trying to see what the cancer looked like. He seemed serenely intrigued by it.

They had reached the big reservoir, under

assault for the past two months from the metal palisades of a future building site. Claude turned his head briefly to the side to ask Gaël to sit back in the seat. The child complied with unpredictable bad grace. His head bumped against the seat and his knee jammed into Simone's back. She turned to smile at him. Already his mood mattered to her and also his opinion of them, although the last half hour had been a struggle and was bringing Claude nothing he had wanted—yet, what had he wanted?—just mounting intolerance to his pain and lost illusions.

Forgetful of his dejection or to dismiss it, Gaël did not sulk for very long. He said that he had come here once before, well, not here exactly, but to the shopping center, and that he had liked it a lot. At home, there was nothing to do, or at least it was a long way away, he insisted with surprising conviction. Then he was silent and they could hear the stealthy rustle as he unwrapped a toffee. Claude shot a swift glance in the rearview mirror. That's enough candy for today, he snapped, like someone forced to repeat himself. Simone observed his flat, almost hollow profile heightened by the tension on his forehead. She could not believe that he was making no effort to win the child's affection, not even him, not even now. Gaël did not flinch. He rolled the toffee noiselessly between his fingers and continued to pull at the paper. Claude was eyeing him but didn't have the strength to put up a fight. He was riled so quickly now but so soon disheartened, and with such weary bitterness. You're too fat for your age, he grunted, as though to himself. Simone looked at him in horror and asked him in an undertone what he was trying to do—teach the boy manners? But Claude took no notice, too intent on watching the little face distorted by chewing the sticky toffee. You're not saying anything, he insisted again, almost triumphant. Gaël turned to the window. I know I'm too fat, he agreed, sucking the syrupy saliva that lapped between his words. His abdication was not enough to satisfy Claude, who went on: Then spit it out. His voice was unbearably pedantic. He's disappointed in the child, thought Simone. People always ended up disappointing him, she realized, with an exultant urge to give in; he only ever loved anyone as a favor.

The sun lit up pearly smears on the windshield where a sponge had been wiped through the pollen dust. Simone shifted her thighs to unstick her dress from the crackling electricity of the seat. The first hot days of spring were making her feel dry and prickly. In the little mirror in front of her, two deep lines formed bitter parentheses in the long, sagging slope of her face. She slipped off the band she had been wearing around her wrist and put her hair up in a ponytail that pulled her features taut. Since the cancer had been diagnosed, she had not dared to go to the hairdresser, and the blond tint was disappearing in her streaky brown-and-gray hair. The idea that there would never again be time to care for her appearance struck her as cruel with the sight in the mirror of this child, who was doing his best to fight off his growing dejection at being with them.

Does your mom still compete? she asked, hugging the headrest under her arm, as though clasping someone familiarly around the neck. The child puffed out his cheeks in a face of astonishment that burst into a smile. It was the first time she had seen him smile, and it pulled his lips right back over his gums, revealing long, wide incisors. She even drives to the bakery, he announced, knocking his head gently against the seat back, his eyes sparkling with fun. His remark sounded like a ritual, a joke that must in some way define her. Repeating it seemed suddenly to reconcile him to his decision to meet them.

They came out opposite the swimming pool, its wall blackened by the swirling shadows of half-erased graffiti. A group of teenagers in track-suits was hanging around the barriers, propped against scooters. They must have been Claude's former pupils, and one of them gave him a little wave, to which Claude responded by raising his chin without taking his eyes off the street. The four heads turned to follow the car and try to catch a glimpse of their strict, condemned teacher, who had said when he left (not that they had reacted, Claude said afterward) that he felt bad about his cancer, like an abdication of responsibility. Simone tried vainly to smile at him, but his expression remained etched on his waxen face. She could not get used to seeing him clam up and not know what to say or do to allay the inevitable terror he still managed to hide, apart from his body's impatience, which guilt and a sudden sense of impotence and humiliation were now exacerbating. Suddenly, for no reason, he announced that he wanted to go home.

Gaël was playing with the seat belt, muffling the clicks in the palm of his hand. No familiarity had been established between them; indeed, his presence in the car seemed increasingly unforgivable. Still toying with the clasp and without looking up, he asked when his mother had said she was coming to pick him up. Simone drew an agonizing breath: That he should lose heart so quickly seemed to her the saddest thing they had had to endure so far.

Claude went upstairs to lie down until the pills took effect, and Gaël took the opportunity to wander off to the bathroom. He came out after some time with dripping bangs and soapy hands, and went to sit down in the living room, wiping damp handprints on his pants. Simone did not know how to ease his embarrassment at finding himself in this intimacy with strangers. Tenderness awoke in her distant and painful inhibitions.

She opened the sliding door to the garden. The insistent roar of a stationary car at the corner of the street drowned out the sounds of spring. Gaël looked around for the television but felt he should not ask to turn it on. Yet the silence was making him uncomfortable. Why had he wanted to meet this father he had known nothing about, who had given him nothing, and why was he anxious to make a good impression? After a moment's hesitation, Simone ventured to ask the question. Gaël limply raised his arms, not because the subject troubled him, but because he must have found it too vast. Then he twisted his mouth to the side before blurting out, in a halfhearted attempt at an explanation, that his mother had always talked about Claude. Simone quietly shrank into her chair to hide the hurt she felt. That was not how things had been presented to her or how she had imagined them. Jovana was a young newlywed when Claude had met and loved her at the tournament abroad. There was no question of a divorce or an abortion. They had decided never to see each other again, to break off all contact and to say no more, and that this was what was best for the child. Claude had lived the whole time with the idea of having done the right thing.

Gaël kicked the thick-cushioned heel of his sneaker against the wood floor as he listened. His pursed lips gave him a strangely sullen air. Claude already told me, he said at last, but anyway, my mother thought it best to tell me when I was little. Simone could sense his eyes darting to and fro behind his lowered lids. She was angry with herself for making him betray Jovana, and she apologized for upsetting him, but he shrugged and smiled with that broad, sudden smile that showed his red gums. He was blessed with a kind of generosity that came out all at once. Simone hated herself for being jealous of a woman who had managed to bring that out in a child. Resentment seldom lasts when you know people, she thought with a pang of sadness. She still wanted to know if Jovana was sorry not to have stayed with Claude, but the question made Gaël skeptical and silent.

You look a lot like him, do you know that? The observation again elicited the wonderful smile. He did not really think so, he said in a pouting voice, his elbows sliding slowly along his thighs. Claude would have thought he should sit up straight, thought Simone a bit pityingly. From the living room, they could see nothing of the houses or of life going on outside, just the lawn and the fragrant snow of the seringas. Gaël no longer knew what to do with himself. He stretched and ran his fingers through his bangs, which had dried stiffly on his forehead; then he scratched his shins through his pants. Mom told me he wouldn't have any hair left, he said at last. His disappointment was thinly masked. Simone stared at him gratefully. She told him that Claude had refused treatment because he didn't want the unnecessary humiliation, since the sickness was so far advanced, and for the first time, his decision struck her as violent disdain for them. Gaël hunched lower and hesitated, then asked if she was sad. He knew from his mother that Claude had been a big smoker. He said it with an air of indulgent reproach and blushed almost as soon as the words were out. Simone tried to change the subject, but Gaël still had things to ask: Why was it Claude's arm that hurt? Did he cry sometimes? Was it true that he was going to die? He let silences open up between his questions, his eyes traveling around the room, looking for something to light on. His hands lay inert between his thighs; they had the glorious plumpness of the rest of his body. Simone could not get enough of watching him, incredulous that it was possible to tell him these things and that he seemed concerned or at least interested. She wished she could have buried her mouth in his extraordinary thick mane of brown hair—the lovely color of a fawn, she told him. Another question was bothering him, but there was the sound of a door upstairs—Claude was coming down. Since he had begun to be in pain and to worry about it, Simone searched his face nervously for his expression whenever he looked at her. Gaël turned sharply toward the hall, as though he, too, were alert to possible fear. His long lashes had stopped beating against his plump cheeks. Simone always kept a box of chocolates in the library; she was sorry she had not given him one when Claude was not looking. She laid a hand on his knee and said she had something to show him in the garden.

Gaël was too small to reach the nest and too heavy to pull himself up by the branches and fence. Simone was afraid that Claude would see his clumsiness. She heard him calling to them. The pain had clearly not subsided, but he was making a point of being with them. Gaël instantly tore himself away from the dense bush, protecting himself from scratches and insects fastidiously. Claude pointed out reproachfully the two anxious blackbirds that were watching from the plum tree. The pillow had left creases on his face, crumpling his severity but doing nothing to soften it. Simone grumbled that he could never loosen up and have a bit of fun. It was sadly obvious that he would never win the child's favor.

Gaël had thought it fun to help make dinner, and Claude did not try to interfere. Simone gave him the lettuce to wash and watched him breaking off leaves in the icy water with immense concentration. His mother would not be long now, and urgency made him talkative. Simone wanted to know what he had been about to ask earlier on, when Claude had come downstairs. Her insistence embarrassed him, and he blushed mischievously. Were you already going out with Claude when he met Mommy? he said, at last. He had finished washing the lettuce and was swirling the residual dirt around in the water. Simone was peeved to think he had heard that from his mother. Her reaction made him shake with a wonderfully throaty laugh, revealing a black hole at the back of his mouth where a tooth had been extracted. Simone wondered what he guessed about her feelings of resentment. She could not bear the thought of his comparing her to his mother and seeing her as old.

Simone spotted the car before he did. She moved away from the window, and her chest constricted with the jealous hurt she had been dreading for several weeks but that now caught her by surprise. Gaël took his time at the sound of the horn. He shook the cold water from his reddened hands and wiped them on his pants. Then he crouched down to retie his laces, stood up, and was about to go to the door but changed his mind and went to kiss her. The spontaneity of his gesture was as genuine as his impatience to leave. In the confusion of their shared embarrassment, their faces missed their mark and Simone had the fleeting surprise of his full lips on the corner of her mouth before they landed squarely on her cheek. She could not help hanging on to his kiss, which he intensified and seemed to infuse with his whole body. I love this child, she thought, watching him run to say good-bye to Claude from the living room door.

The door slammed shut, and Simone saw him reach the garden gate in a few joyful bounds.

Before he dived into the car, he took a last look (but failed to see her) over the hood. Jovana was also looking toward the house without seeing her. She was not very different from the way she looked in the photo Claude had kept of her, standing young and radiant in jogging pants on a podium. Her bangs were combed down as they had been then, very low and straight on her face, with its high, round cheekbones split by an enormous red smile. She was wearing a light gray hooded sweatshirt, and a high ponytail of thick russet-brown hair just like Gaël's was bobbing above it. The SUV was enormous and had a stripe all down one side. A sticker warned that there were children on board. Simone had not even asked whether Gaël had brothers and sisters. It was only later, when she was setting the table, that Claude told her Jovana had brought him up alone for more than nine years. He refused to add anything at that point. His face looked like wax and was completely gray. It was crazy to think that he and Jovana had ever coupled.

Cédric had not introduced himself, and his *Yes?* rang loud and false through the receiver. Simone reached out to push the study door shut. The electric blinds were lowered, and light from the street clawed fine grooves into the darkness that had fallen around her. Claude was not in bed. She waited to see if he would pick up the phone in the bedroom, but nothing, not even a hello. He was leaving them to deal with all comment.

Is he really my brother? Cédric asked with an awkward little laugh. Simone said yes. The reaction took time coming and surprised her by its neutrality. He wanted to know if it had gone okay, whether his father had been overly upset. Yolande must have been standing beside him, holding Aude, and the little girl's whimpers were suddenly audible through the receiver. Cédric muffled the mouthpiece for a moment, then returned to the call and apologized, sounding oddly annoyed.

He was a teenager when Gaël was born and was living with his mother, who had already separated from Claude years before, though she was still concerned enough to have been kept up-to-date and to have thought that Jovana was trying to use him. Cédric, too, had thought his father naïve. The annoyance of being wrong added to the distress caused by his father's sickness and must have struck him as just as arbitrary and unfair. Like his father, he was not good either at offering comfort or opening up. Simone had often marveled that Yolande, whose sweet, blond features were a painful excitement to men, had settled for a frustrating husband. Cédric was celebrating his sixteenth birthday when Simone had met him. She had thought him pleasant but uninspiring, despite his wonderful gray eyes. He had come across as polite and serious, anxious to appear glad to meet her. Simone had been going out with Claude for a few months. Their relationship was not earth-shattering, but it was genuine. Above all, it was joyless, as she had realized at that birthday celebration, watching his tall, oddly formal son helping to clear the table, shoulders hunched. She had wept about it in a panic of lucidity, staring wide-eyed and haggard at her reflection in the bedroom mirror upstairs while Cédric watched the news with his father in silence, waiting until it was time for his train. She had moved in with Claude shortly afterward and tried to believe in their happiness regardless, but she had never warmed to Cédric. Something about him deterred affection, perhaps the adult displays of care he showed for Claude, who had been shattered by a messy divorce he had not wanted. Until he was eighteen, he had devoted every other Sunday to them, escaping the dingy backdrop of the neighborhood by going out for long bike rides with his father. Simone was aware that it was Claude who had been hampered by this routine. Cédric had been snatched from him prematurely and for a long time. The efforts necessary to enforce his visiting rights had turned out to be the best thing Claude had to give. His attachment was simply a matter of guilt, and Simone guessed that, ultimately, that was what had made the separation acceptable.

Cédric was less interested in Gaël than in the situation. Simone was happy she did not have to tell him that she had liked the little boy. She was angry with herself for being moved by such affection, for the warmth of her feelings was gradually dissolving her courage of recent months. Cédric wanted to know what Claude had in mind with this kid, whether he hoped to be loved by him before he died, and if he was expecting them to act as his family. Simone at least had to allow him that: his lucidity was more charitable than Claude's guilt. A car had just drawn up a few meters away alongside the hedge. Simone held the receiver away from her ear to listen to car doors slamming and voices echoing disproportionately in the dark. Outside in the garden, watched over by the towering apartment buildings and barricaded shopping center, the noises sounded more threatening, as though squeezed up against the ludicrous plastic screen of the roller shutters. Simone had never been aware of her fears before Claude fell sick; explaining them demanded an energy that now seemed too dispersed. She told Cédric that she would rather continue their conversation about all that tomorrow when she and Claude went over to see them. The car had driven off and silence had fallen heavily about her by the time she hung up.

She went into the living room to raise the electric blinds. Slowly, the night and hedges appeared, split by light from the streetlamps. Beyond the cluster of round paving stones, the lawn stretched like black water. The air was still and fresh, sweet with the scent of mock orange. Simone had only just realized that she would probably have to live here on her own afterward, at least for a while, until she had found something to do and somewhere to go. Dread wrung a groan from her. The blinds of two neighboring houses were lowered on total silence. In the distance, toward the city center, a rotating light ground into the night's cloudy vastness. Simone walked over to the forsythia, lit to transparency by the blinding glare of a porch bulb. The female was there with her feathers all spread out and her beak poking over the edge of the nest like a thorn. Simone parted the branches to get closer and wondered how long the bird's fortitude would hold out. This instant of cruelty absorbed her just long enough for the feeling of panic to abate and let her breathe. She withdrew gingerly from the aggressive tangle of branches. Claude's face was glued to the window of Cédric's old room. He had gotten up and switched on the light when he heard someone moving around in the garden. He had grown fearful, too, now that pain had left him with no hold on his body. Simone waved to him to go back to bed and went in without shutting the blinds behind her. He was the one who insisted they barricade themselves in; she had never gotten used to the oppression of the rooms behind their flimsy plastic defenses. Loneliness, she reflected, brought with it the return of these little liberties.

Simone turned out the light in the hallway and waited for her eyes to get used to the thick, heavy darkness of the bedroom. Claude was not asleep. A move under the sheets raised the new, irksome odor of the bed, where he lay distant and frozen, battling with his horror at the slightest contact, the smallest expression of concern. Simone would not get to sleep while she felt him tense and hostile despite himself. It was as though they had turned into thistles for each other. His apprehension of her was the only outward sign of the onset of death. Simone knew the exact spot beneath his left shoulder blade where the pain had first started up. There was no seeing it and no reaching it, however much she pressed as he first asked her to, embarrassed to find himself worried—really worried—and bizarrely offended. The word *cancer* had been a relief to him, since he had at least not been wrong in insisting about the pain. On the X-rays, the milky shadow smudged out the top of his left lung and spread over the pleura and ribs. Claude was irritable and taciturn when he came home from his hospital appointments. He had put up with it for too long and now there was no hope; his one aim was to hurtle to the end as fast as possible. He gave them no option and refused to discuss it. His intolerance of pity and questions was nasty. Simone no longer knew how to love him properly, or, indeed, how to love him at all, and there was no one around to whom she could admit that she had started to resent him for it. The memory of Gaël's affection and the way he had kissed her with his whole face planted firmly against her cheek continued to make her tingle. Soundlessly, she began to cry about her physical loneliness, imagining that it would be forever.

You didn't shut the living room blinds. The rebuke broke the silence abruptly, like a dry cough. Simone countered it with slow, regular breathing, as though she were asleep. Tears rolled into her mouth and over her neck. She dared not suggest moving into a separate room, and he would never admit that the presence of his partner in bed with him was unbearable for his body, for his anxiety about death, and maybe, too, for his guilt at abandoning her. Simone wondered how long you could share a painful space guarded against you with such hostility.

CÉDRIC HAD LEFT the gate open to the narrow brick house and the walled garden, now completely white with blossoming fruit trees. He was on the phone, picking absently at bubbles of green paint that were flaking off with rust. Claude gave a little hoot that jerked him upright, like a slap, out of the slouch brought on by the boredom of waiting. The maneuver to get into the yard without scraping against the walls of the alleyway was clumsy. Still on the phone, Cédric eyed him closely. But it was really the expression on Claude's face, drawn by concentration and pain, that he was watching. It caused him deep, overwhelming anxiety to see his father suffer, but he found no other means of expressing it than through this total seriousness. He had put on weight in recent months and his shoulders and thighs filled out his city clothes with confident solidity. Simone was always struck by how conscientiously he played the adult he had been so eager to become.

They had bought the house shortly before Yolande had given birth; brambles had invaded the planks and rubble intended for alterations that had never come to fruition. As she stood up out of the car, Simone felt her foot come down on a plastic figurine, which she sent into the bushes, her eyes on Yolande, who was coming toward them from the garden at Aude's tottering pace. She smiled at them from her blond, supremely delicate features and called out *Hello* and *How are you?* Claude waved back and slowly extricated himself from his seat. She must have thought him changed, because tears rose to her eyes, glistening and surprising. Simone had heard her sob the day the news of the cancer had broken. She was suspicious of these displays of emotion: her own pain had been slow to be released. She stepped forward to take Aude in her arms and warn Yolande under her breath that things weren't great. The little girl's warmth as she trustingly crumpled against her breast almost wrung a moan from her, so tense was she from Claude's mood that morning. At breakfast, he had dropped a cup. Things were slipping away from him; he was starting to lose his sense of feeling, and again, there had been no way of talking about it. Not even Gaël's arrival had elicited comment, and it was too late to say anything now without embarrassment or tension.

Cédric took Claude into the house, his arm around his father's shoulder in a gesture of newfound intimacy that was terribly awkward.

Yolande waited for the door to close behind them. So, is it true, Gaël looks like him? she asked after a moment's hesitation, with the same edgy laugh Cédric had given the day before on the phone. Simone replied that she adored him without elaborating, because that was the truth and she didn't think she needed to spare the couple's happiness. Yolande listened to her, stroking her daughter's hair, so fair that it was almost white. She could not understand why no one had tried to make contact with Jovana during all those years. A truculent frown appeared on her forehead, a kind of old rebellion against them or a determination to think her own thoughts, which Simone would never have suspected her of. As happened so often, Simone blamed herself for not being able to love her.

Attention was focused mostly on the little girl during mealtimes, and Claude was happy to go along with not being expected to take part. In any case, he coped better with his impatience at the pain in gatherings than in one-on-ones. Simone thought with a pang that she had only ever shared with Gaël the distress his abruptness caused her. The incident with the cup that morning preyed on her till she felt she would choke. It was a symptom they had expected, and it presaged the start of the worst. She resented Claude for his ability to bluff.

It wasn't his way to take the floor, and his voice was probably less firm than he would have liked when he announced over coffee that he had finally decided to undergo treatment. Cédric froze, and Yolande, who had Aude on her lap, seemed to shrink into the baby's soft body. Claude had been so determined and convincing in his rejection of a pointless battle that this U-turn forced them, without warning, to face their awareness that they were waiting for him to die. He stared down at his folded hands on the cloth, anxious to soothe or conceal any telltale signs on his face. Jovana couldn't handle the little boy, he had inferred, and he was ashamed of giving up; that was all. He thought he was being a coward, a disgrace. Cédric looked now at Simone now at his wife, whose eyes grew big with tears. He seemed to be seeking support for his revolt. Whereas we, we're not worth wanting to live for, he said sardonically, rolling up his napkin while Yolande got up from the table with the baby in her arms. Claude made a face to dismiss the remark. You're not the ones with anything to complain about. It was said without pity or compassion for the pain he was inflicting, or maybe just with no thought for them. Simone sat leaning forward with her hands on her thighs. Nothing but a groan could have passed her lips. The idea of having to go back, in reverse, along the way they had come to reach his decision not to accept treatment appalled her. She would not have the courage for a long illness that would not get better. She had just enough courage for a few months, she kept saying to herself, trying calmly to pile up the plates. Claude fell silent when he saw her get up, and he apologized for not having spoken to her about it sooner. To her amazement, Simone found she was not even capable of anger.

Yolande turned around when she heard Simone enter the kitchen. Her whole face was stammering with incomprehension. Why didn't he ever listen to us? she sputtered unhappily. Simone could not fathom why Yolande needed to feel she mattered to her father-in-law. She envied Yolande her ability to think about him, when all she felt was self-pity. There was a scraping of chairs; then the front door banged shut with a loud rattle of windowpanes. Yolande put her head into the hallway, looking disoriented and guilty at her resentment. But Cédric was already coming to join them, a clutch of glasses in either hand, motioning that everything was all right. He's waiting in the car for you, he told Simone, raising his eyebrows in irritation and surprise at Yolande's tears.

At least now we know how much we're loved, he sneered icily. What does he think he can do for them, come back to life? He had cut a slice of bread and chewed it, staring at them in turn in bewilderment and distress. Simone gripped the back of the high chair to calm her dizziness; her face was burning, and her eyes were smarting as though she had grit in them. She described the incident that morning—how Claude was starting to lose control of his left hand—as if trying to find an excuse for his driving. The idea that he could no longer see how close he was to his own death traumatized her. She felt as though she was going off with a madman.

Cédric's revolt had washed over her in an instant, like rising bile she was unable to vomit up, just a trickle of saliva. The bathroom looked straight out among the branches of the fruit trees. All that sparkling whiteness clouded with the tears she dabbed at hopelessly, ordering herself to get a grip. Life with Claude had been safe, stable, and frustrating. For a long time, pleasure had come from seeing him abandon himself for her sake to an intimacy that somehow offended him. He had never gone in for the effusions she had hoped for; his lovemaking had been earnest and hurried, always vaguely embarrassed, and she had resented him without admitting it to herself, never truly fulfilled but neither telling him nor forgiving him, and, above all, without understanding that so little did not satisfy him, either. We didn't give each other enough happiness, she kept mumbling uncontrollably to herself while Yolande tapped anxiously at the door and Aude, left on her own downstairs, began to wail.

On that day of extraordinary radiance and spring growth tumbling into the heavy caress of the Seine, the return home and the approach of the shopping center on the horizon, where the tower blocks loomed in fours over the old villages, struck Simone like an assault. She felt as though she was entering a fog of depression, forsaken and silent, from which Claude had always refused, during all these years, to break free and go and live somewhere else. He's been so stubborn, and for what? she thought. Who's it helped, staying put? Her tears began to fall again. She didn't bother to hide them, and leaned her head against the car window, screwing up her handkerchief into a hard crumpled ball in her fist. Claude was just going to have to get used to seeing her cry, since there was not an ounce of courage to hope for from her. He was silent. For a few minutes, a scooter had been keeping pace with the car, letting a gap open up, then looping around them again with a casual swing of the rider's slumped back. Each time, the helmeted head turned its blank face to them, revealing nothing but the reflections of the traffic passing across the opaque visor. Could Claude put a name to the body? He had known them all intimately under their flapping short pants and T-shirts, in effort and the hard, wild freedom of youth. Simone did not understand what this car chase was about. She was afraid of smoldering resentments kindled by the assault at the sports club. What does he want from you? she asked with a virulence that surprised her. There was a kind of flicker in Claude's eyes when he turned to her. Her comment had distracted or annoyed him. They had reached the turn into their street and could see smoke rising from it and hear a crackling fire of branches. Claude turned the wheel slowly as he entered the street. His mouth was twisted in bitterness. The only thing bothering him the whole time had been the whims of his lazy hand, Simone realized.

After the garage door had swung to behind the car and Claude had switched off the engine, he looked at her, grasped her shoulder and gave her a gentle shake, and said, I'm sorry, then begged her to pull herself together and got out. Simone watched him straighten up under the concrete ceiling oozing long trickles of saltpeter. The roof window cut a disk of sunlight among the dust and spiderwebs. Claude walked over to take a look, perhaps checking that the scooter had disappeared, and it was at that moment that something in his suffering finally buckled.

She had never seen him weep. His sobs gave him an oddly frowning expression that embarrassed her. He put his numb hand up to his face, vainly stuck two fingers in his wet eyes, then wiped his mouth on his sleeve. It took Simone a few seconds to understand and to accept the regrets that washed over him. It was so incredibly cruel and so sudden that she could not even find the strength to evade his shivering embrace. She would never manage either to forgive him or to console him for having wanted to see Jovana again, she realized.

It was twelve minutes past four, displayed in red digits that swam in the pitch-black of the bedroom. Claude was no longer in bed; the imprint of chilled sweat left a totally dark presence, and Simone ran her hand over it, trying calmly to fend off her distress and disgust. The wind whistled and echoed along the gutters, startling the night with a strange tension. But it took Simone some time to get worried about what Claude was doing, force herself out of her leaden tiredness, and throw on a bathrobe.

He had put the light on in the sitting room. The net curtains were half turned back and behind them the slats of the fragile gray screen were packed together. A glass of water and a yogurt container had been left out on the coffee table. The sound of the television was off, and a passing high-speed train majestically crossed the picture. Simone turned up the volume; then she switched the TV off and called out to Claude. He was nowhere to be found: he had gone out into the street.

Simone saw him in the distance, standing in the middle of the street, legs astride like a guard. The loneliness of the neighborhood was heavy with darkness and perfumes stirred by the gales. Mist shimmered way off downtown, where the bar of buildings formed a black rectangle dotted with glinting staircases. A few dozen meters away, the traffic seemed to be coming at them off the freeway out of a void of thick silence; that was where Claude was looking. Simone could not bring herself to call him. The sight of him standing in the street in his pajamas derailed her with pity. It scared her far more to see him behaving suddenly irrationally than to know he was done for.

He stood there motionless for a few minutes; then his back relaxed, he shook his painful arm, took a good look around, and then turned seeming not a bit surprised to see her. Simone shrank into a corner of the hallway, groping for something to steady her confusion. The garden gate swung closed with a metallic clunk; then she heard the shuffle of slippers along the passage, and suddenly Claude was there under the crude light in the hall. He was getting up early. It was ages since Simone had seen him in the slovenly state of waking. Strands of hair, which he had always worn in a stiff gray brush, were crushed down against the sides of his head; his cheeks were hollow under the stubble and his thin lips seemed to have been fused by a chalk line. His body still looked fit but somehow dulled by the invisible ash of cancer. He's dying, she realized, for the first time fully aware of this.

There was another attack against a bus, he announced, closing the door behind him. Simone said, Oh yes, and waited for him to go on. It was in C., you know, farther east, but I just had to go and see. See what? she asked softly, thinking, What on earth was he hoping to put right? See what could be done was his irritated rejoinder, brought out with an aggressive expression of pain. Simone tightened the belt of her robe without answering. His pain would always be impenetrable to her, but his sudden fears and his outrageous sensitivities, and now this kind of illogicality, were seeping into her like poison.

For as long as she had known him, he had been a volunteer firefighter but had been called out no more than twice, the first time to put out a blazing shed, the second time to watch a detached house collapse with an old man and his dog trapped inside. If something happened, he would not be called—people in the area must already know that he was no longer in a fit state. His eyes scanned her harshly, as though defying her to think, like the others, that he was finished. Simone could feel the edge of the door frame digging into her spine; she felt like falling on the floor, wailing and begging him to get real.

A car went by in an explosion of bass notes; then it was dark again, and quiet and windy. Claude was not sleepy; he put the kettle on and got out the biscuits. They both sat down at the kitchen table. Street lighting through the branches of the birch tree shifted cheerfully on the ceiling. Claude stretched out his arm to take the kettle and pour water over the tea bags in the cups. The twisted collar of his pajama top gaped over his ashen neck, where warts stood out on minuscule threads of skin. Simone could not remember when these growths had first appeared; they played on her mind unhappily. She gathered her robe about her, from which escaped a fishy waft of sleep. How pathetic two adult bodies are, alone in the night when all desire is gone. Gradually, shame gave way to sorrow. Jovana's half-glimpsed youth merged with the memory of the little boy's kiss in the same feeling of inevitable jealousy.

Claude took little slurps, pushing out his lips in a moist pout. Simone pointed out that they had not even talked about Gaël, but the look he cast her over his cup was absent. She added that she had adored him and wished she had never met him. Claude was still not listening. He had taken off his slippers and was staring at his bare feet, which lay flat on the tiled floor. My left foot feels as though it's touching the floor through a sock, he noted after a moment. A half smile floated on his lips, a smile of bitter satisfaction. It was time I decided to get treatment, he went on, laying his hand on hers in a ghastly protective gesture. Simone stared at him, not daring to understand that he genuinely wanted to get better, cursing love, or desire, that had spawned such crazy, reckless hope. She said, Yes, sure, and smiled at him, her chest tight with screams she could not release. The sickness was getting worse, but it would now be she who was in pain. We weren't carefree, but we were happy all the same, mostly because we respected each other, she mused, watching him put his slippers back on. From now on, we're going to lie to each other.

JOVANA CALLED a bit over a month after that night when the gales had broken off the tops of the birch and when Claude, for the first time in ten years, had not come back to bed. Simone answered the call, while he tried to keep down his nausea on the sofa. She took him the receiver and he grabbed it from her, adopting a suspicious, almost irritated look, which mostly made Simone feel offended. The room went suddenly dark with the rustling approach of a shower of fine rain falling vertically on the lawn. Claude stood up from the sofa to close the French doors. His whole body was angled toward Jovana's voice, and he answered her repeatedly with a marked *Right*. Simone watched him sit back down on the edge of the sofa, his bad hand upturned on his thigh like a dead beetle. Having her listening to him was putting him off, and she eventually obeyed his almost pleading awkwardness and went back to her work. The study window looked out on a great shaft of sunshine through dazzling white streaks of rain. Simone sat down to face the prescriptions, checks, and patients' notes piled neatly on either side of the computer. She finished the cold dregs of a coffee and kicked the door shut so as not to overhear anything. The pain of jealousy sucked her mind into a great hole of anxiety. She could think of nothing other than the dwindling hope of what love was left. It was the only sorrow she was capable of: an incurable bitterness that she was not even loved enough by Claude to be able to be of any use to him.

Claude half-sat up on the sofa when he heard her come back into the room. The purple rings around his eyes gave him the wild stare of a convict. Jovana was hoping they could have Gaël stay with them for a week or two. She had to go to Belgrade and couldn't take him with her. Her scruples were genuine, he insisted, massaging the back of his neck with both hands, and the request so legitimate, he couldn't exactly protest that he was tired and throwing up. Simone waited for him to say straight out that he had agreed. She eyed him, his wasted body swamped in the folds of his tracksuit, the receiver lying between his legs like a kind of unseemly outsize penis. She was finding the submissive way that he was letting the treatment wear him down, irascibly and stubbornly hopeful, so difficult to cope with. Did he really think that he could put up with the absurd added torture, in front of the little boy, of knowing that Jovana was happy? Still, Simone tried to convince herself that at least these artificial duties would take his mind off the nausea his days reeled by in, and the paralysis that was gradually anesthetizing the pain but which was not yet more than loss of feeling. The previous day, an unsightly bald patch the size of a medallion had appeared on the back of his head where his hair had fallen out. The sight of this ivory crust caught her off guard every time with a wave of nausea and had the bizarre effect of tarnishing the memory of Gaël. Claude, of course, had not managed to describe to Jovana the hell of silent patience the stay would be for an eleven-year-old child. They ought to have called her back to warn her, but Simone did not know how or where to reach her. Gaël didn't want to talk to me on the phone, Claude added suddenly, getting up to take the remote control. His delayed amazement was full of bitterness and foreboding, and it unhinged her. She felt cowardly for not daring to tell him that he couldn't look after the child in this condition, and guilty for looking forward so crazily to being with and helped by a bit of youth.

IT HAD BEEN AGREED that Jovana would bring Gaël on Saturday toward midday. In the morning, Simone flung open the door to the garden, hoping to let out the chemo-thickened air and cloying staleness of flaking skin. The sitting room was bright with a fine early-summer light. The heat was creeping over the lawn, rousing a buzzing of wasps among the heavy bunches of plums, which looked like hard kernels. Simone brought out the plastic seats but couldn't find where the umbrella was kept. Expectation was throwing her into a kind of impotence. She had left Claude huddled, shivering, over the toilet, exhausting himself to tears as he strained vainly to expel the stones that were lacerating his anus. His troubles affected her but left her no possibility for reaction or sympathy.

It was not quite twelve o'clock when the dark form of the SUV glided slowly up behind the hedge to the gate. Simone had gone back to watching the street from the kitchen window. She felt her heart bump and thought how crazy she was to be so nervous and fearful.

There was a little involuntary hoot; then the

car radio stopped, all the windows rose together, and half-glimpsed faces were eclipsed by the reflection of the roofs against the deep blue summer sky. In the long, motionless minute that followed, Simone's joy began to falter, sapped by the trivial fact of Claude's silence, for he was still locked in the lavatory. Jovana had just squeezed through the half-open garden gate and was squinting into the sun. Simone had not expected her to be tall. Jovana's punctuality inexplicably disarmed her jealousy.

Jovana was wearing a bright blue flared miniskirt over black leggings stretched so tight that they were almost transparent on her sturdy thighs, and chunky white sneakers. Her hair was pulled back in a high ponytail the same as before, her face was full and glowing, and her whole build gave her a virile but girlish mien, with brisk, healthy gestures that were instantly beguiling. Gaël had gotten out of the car, too, but was still engrossed in an electronic game, his body limply blocking the open gate. Simone could see the tousled movement of his hair on the back of his neck, rubbed up the whole journey against the seat back. Jovana had taken a big backpack out of the trunk and was peering shortsightedly at the house. She asked Gaël several times with a kind of numb patience to get a move on and clear up the mess and to stop *that thing*. Simone shouted up to Claude that they had arrived, but she got no reply. So she made up her mind to go and open the door, not sorry to have to see and feel right away, fully and unrelieved, the regret one might have for not being with a woman like that.

Jovana did a double take of surprise when she saw her at the front door. Her full lips were sucked in with the same mannerism Simone had loved in Gaël. Jovana said hello and held out her hand, then changed her mind and offered her cheek for a kiss. Simone found she smelled of fries and Nivea. She felt mean-spirited, hurt. Gaël came forward in his turn for a kiss, but he was scratching his elbow angrily and refused to meet her gaze. Everything about him suggested sullen resentment of his mother. Jovana looked him up and down without taking offense at his sulking or showing any real sympathy. I really can't take him, she explained again with a smile, gesturing vaguely toward the reason she had given on the phone. She had picked up a snail shell and threw it into the flowers, jolting the backpack off her shoulder. I've put in some gym clothes, she said by way of asking about Claude's condition. Simone replied, flabbergasted, that there was absolutely no question of his doing any sports. Jovana's oversight had aroused Simone's anxieties about what they were going to do with the child for two weeks. She nearly said that it would no longer be possible, but Claude was standing at the foot of the stairs with his hand on the rail, as though stopped in his tracks as he was about to go back upstairs.

He had given up the tracksuit for a shirt and corduroy trousers, rubbed the stale odor of his lusterless skin with toilet water, and shaved off what remained of his brush of hair, which had fallen out, leaving great patches as pale as wax. Simone was seeing for the first time, and together with Jovana, his somehow enormous, hairless scalp, cast from the same dented bone as his face. What had he thought as he checked his appearance in the mirror? Had he been hoping for something? Had he seen that he had turned into somebody else, someone with a crazed, oddly younger, almost disquieting look?

Jovana shot him a warm, slightly commiserating hello. Nothing was left of the love she had felt twelve years earlier except an obvious intimate sadness at not recognizing him like this, a sadness that would pass or come out as nostalgia, and Claude, lucid and stiff, registered this, looking around for Simone with a kind of silent, unbearably pathetic supplication. Gaël stood in anxious and awkward surprise at the sight of the drab face and yellow scalp. Yielding to a sympathetic intuition, he seized the backpack and took Claude's hand to follow him upstairs to his bedroom.

It was the room they called Cédric's and it had always been used as a storeroom to keep bottles of water and boxes of old papers. It was over the study and opposite their own room, and it looked straight across at the neighbors' bedroom, where the window was blocked up, in summer and winter alike, by a cloth of turquoise batik. Claude had ended the first nights of his nausea in this room. He would not be able to take refuge here for two weeks. Simone dreaded the intimacy that would have to be reappropriated in an increasingly sensitive discomfort. Neither of them had dared to own up to their apprehensions as they straightened up the room to make it look more or less welcoming.

Gaël jumped onto the bed on his knees and hung right out of the open window over the green tangle of forsythia. He could see the street when he leaned out completely, he called out loudly, as though hoping for an echo. His T-shirt rode up and his paunchy hips mushroomed over the low waistline of his pants. In the sunshine, his hair was a dark fiery red. Simone thought he looked a bit older than the first time. He did not seem to fit in this child's room, shrunk to a passageway between the piles of boxes draped with sheets. She told him that he was making her dizzy leaning out like that, but he wasn't listening. So she kicked an escaping plastic crate back under the bed and sat down on the edge of the mattress. Gaël sank back on his heels. His face was flushed, and he rubbed it up and down vigorously for a moment with the flat of his hands, as if to get rid of something bothering him. His bangs stuck up a bit comically in a quiff over his raised eyebrows. What was your name again? he asked suddenly with a hint of impudence. I forgot. Simone told him but did not take her eyes off him, unhinged to realize that he was already reckoning exactly how he could take advantage of her attachment to him. In fact, he was not really the way she remembered him. Nevertheless, she felt a wave of affection that took her breath away.

The backpack had toppled over at the end of the bed. Gaël bent down to stand it up but failed and sat down again, oddly breathless from the effort. He cast a look around at the piles of boxes; then his shoulders drooped slightly. He said twice that, the day he first came, he hadn't seen that there was a child's room. His voice sounded edgy, suggesting he'd had a nervous week that Simone felt guilty for. She wondered if he was aware and was peeved at how selfish they all were.

Jovana was standing in the corridor with Claude, leaning back against the handrail with the slightest contortion of embarrassment. Simone heard her asking how the treatment was going, carefully wording her sentences to avoid sounding either too formal or too familiar. It was fascinating how alien they were to each other and yet how true the tenderness remained. Then, finding nothing to say that had not been said the first time—the rest would have needed more time and intimacy than Jovana was probably ready to give—she gave his arm a sisterly rub and went to say good-bye to her son.

Gaël made a hopeful but prudent move when he saw her bounce in and crush her lips against his, gently rubbing their faces together. The transgressive panache of their kiss drove Simone out. She got up from the bed and left the room but was pulled up short by the surprise of seeing Claude's unrecognizable head again, his huge forehead now wrinkled in confusion almost to the top of his skull. The noise of a lawn mower filled the rooms. The front door's been left open, she said, hurtling down the stairs in panic and distress.

Claude followed her, and a few seconds later

Jovana came down herself, probably aware and worried that she had caused offense. Her dimpled face appeared at the kitchen door. A gift was clutched under the plump flesh of her bare crossed arms. Gaël had stayed in his room and shouted down to her to look up at the window when she went out. He did not want to come down, although she insisted, and set up a lazy whining, which she dismissed with a pretty, careless toss of her head, turning to tell Claude that he shouldn't let himself be bossed around. She obviously had no idea what she was rousing in them. Simone was touched to see the pads of pink flesh bulging over her nails, which were bitten down to the quick. She felt stupidly fragile, unable to quell the unjustified resentment that had gotten the better of her.

Jovana took a step forward to put the present on the table. I'll be going, then, she announced to the interminable silence. Simone nodded. She could see Claude in the background, standing ignored in the darkening corridor. Finally, he disappeared. His absurd head brought tears to her eyes. What she really found unbearable was the ease with which he faced down this humiliation.

A trickle of salt was choking her. I'm sorry, I'm stupid, she just about managed to get out, tapping her lips with two fingers as though to relieve a burning mouth. Jovana glanced briefly toward the sitting room, where Claude's figure was dwindling into the dazzling light from the garden. I'll take Gaël back with me. I hadn't realized things had gotten so bad. Her intonation was cheerful; it wasn't a blunder, but a perfectly adult, graceful observation. But it pained her to give up her plans, and the faintest hint of disappointment had extinguished the warmth in her face. Simone assured her that it would be all right, that she would find a way of keeping Gaël busy if Claude felt too tired. Making an effort to be generous comforted her sense of emptiness and loss. She could not, in any case, imagine going back to being alone with Claude after having had the hope of a bit of life in the house. Jovana turned around as though to make sure Claude approved, but he was still standing facing the garden. The sun had left the lawn and the room, and his listless presence seemed increasingly ominous. Simone suddenly could no longer stand the state of submission he was reduced to by the treatment, or the sorrow, or both. Go now, she said, turning away.

Jovana jotted down her mobile number on a scrap of paper and left it beside the gift, insisting they call her if things weren't going well. Simone closed the door without answering. There was nothing that could be said without bitterness or too much blameworthy, pointless emotion. She walked over to the open window so as not to hear them saying good-bye and, above all, not to sense him floundering so expressively. The lawn mower had stopped. A warm breeze filled the room with the rustle of leaves. The street lay in the white heat of weekend peace. Opposite, the shutters had been closed for two weeks. An unclipped rosebush cast long purple stems over the gate; at night, a hall light stayed on, probably to deter vandals, forming a round crisscrossed eye. They barely knew anyone now in the neighborhood. A lot of people had left, put off by the encroaching city and the fear of gangs. There had been scuffles and disagreements. Claude could not forgive people fleeing from a world they had allowed to degenerate. Simone could scarcely remember the morally involved man he had once been. He had been let down, had gotten tired of understanding, and had sent everyone back to their grudges with the bitter disgust that was killing him. The realization of their isolation suddenly gave her a hollow feeling. She hardly dared imagine the sense of failure and futility Claude must have to confront during the precarious silences of his illness.

Gaël's voice echoed along the hallway, as

though sucked out through the open front door. Jovana was off at last. She went down the two front steps and looked back up at the window, shielding her eyes against the brightness of the sky. Her face was once more full of eager anticipation at going away. She blew him a kiss and promised to call every day, then disappeared in a flash of blue.

A red car screeched to a halt beside the SUV, its tinted windows jarring like blind eyes in the midday light. Jovana watched it reverse and advance several times in a kind of weirdly aggressive dance that didn't seem to make her hesitate. Claude had not closed the door, and Simone felt the call of a draft through the house. She wondered what about him, Jovana, or the SUV had made the car stop. Gaël's voice was no longer to be heard. But he was still at the window, probably sulking, because Jovana was frowning with a pout of gentle annoyance as she turned to the gate to call out a last good-bye. The car had vanished and a great empty silence descended on them. Jovana craned her neck to scan the end of the street and threw her bag on the passenger seat. Then her bobbing ponytail slapped the edge of the car roof and the door closed behind her. She took a while to get going. It dawned on Simone that she was probably leaving her son for the first time and that, however pressing the reason, at this moment she must be blaming herself for it.

Simone waited a few minutes before going to see what Claude was doing. She found him sitting at the table in the living room, his head turned to the garden, where the wind was catapulting unripe but already shriveled plums onto the lawn. His fingers were gingerly feeling the top of his scalp. Simone suddenly saw what he had found: a deep round scar, like a hole made with the point of a pencil. She noticed, too, that his feet were bare in nearly new deck shoes she had never seen him wear before. His sadness offended her, tortured her; she could figure it out only too well. Gaël's silence upstairs was weighing on them like an accusation. She would have liked to ask him to come and help her make lunch, but she didn't dare. His grumpiness intimidated her. Above all, she did not feel the same freedom, now that she no longer really recognized him, now that it was totally unthinkable not to find ways to endear him to them.

It was that evening when they tried to console themselves by making love, but Claude's body would not respond. He apologized, hugging her awkwardly to his bony frame with its odor of rancid talcum powder. Morphine was casting the same somnolence over his pain and his instincts, although he had obeyed them all these years, comforting them with the regularity of their transports. Simone was in a state of vague arousal from blighted tenderness and fatigue but was not necessarily looking for satisfaction. She said it didn't matter and closed her eyes. In truth, she was afraid he would think he had to say he loved her and would want to kiss her. She recoiled at the idea; his unhealthy saliva reminded her of chewed chalk.

It was still early. Dusk outside was visible through the blinds that hung in the thick warmth of the room. They had gone to bed at the same time as Gaël, disrupted out of their routine and strangely uneasy on this first evening, which they had weakly frittered away in front of the television. His presence on the other side of the landing recalled former weekends with Cédric. Eight years had gone by without anything jogging their memory. And now Claude's body was no longer capable of love, and now the hand resting on her hip was touching her through a thick glove without feeling.

Simone was hot; her leg between his was tingling. Feeling her disentangling herself, Claude apologized again, rubbed her arm, and turned over. The silence in the room was oppressive.

Before long, it was split by a whistle from the street, alerting them to the low thrum of stationary cars with their engines running beneath their windows, probably for a while.

The district emptied out during the holidays and had become a meeting place for dealers, some of whose faces Claude probably recognized. Simone's heart sank when she saw him sit up on the edge of the bed. It was, in a way, his failure he was going out to contemplate. What are you going to do? she asked, rolling over on her back, pressing her hands over her eyes.

Claude went over to the window to peer through the gaps in the blinds. That red car is there again, he announced with odd impatience, and left the room. He stumbled away into the dark silence of the house. Simone sat up in bed and seemed to see its pale shape floating in the room. At least tonight, she thought with bitter relief, we won't have to swallow the hair that falls out in handfuls. It was crazy the things one could come to look out for and put up with without complaining.

There was a sudden burst of engines revving and people shouting down below. Car doors banged and headlights briefly swept away down the street just as Claude was putting the porch light on. Simone heard him open the door, then rattle the rusty handle on the garden gate. As peace returned, the sounds reached her so clearly, she felt they were right beside her. She pictured to herself his naked scalp under the halo of street-lights. She felt so depressed by his restless urge to be out in the world again that she almost went down to join him.

Claude had reached their door, when he changed his mind and crossed the landing to Gaël's room. Simone put one foot out of bed. The boy was leaning out of the window and must have been watching the cars maneuvering as he peered through the leaves of the silver birch. He turned around when he heard someone come in. His expression of surprise at the light was distorted by excitement. Claude went over to him, probably to ask him what he had seen. Gaël listened in silence, his buttocks squeezed between his heels. Simone guessed immediately that he was about to lie.

THE CAR HAD CRASHED and one of the passengers had been killed that night, but they did not find out till much later in the day. It was still early; it was fresh and calm and the garden was drenched in shade under a pale, milky sky. At dinner the previous day, Claude had suggested that Gaël accompany him on his morning walk to the stadium, but all he got in reply was a shyly obstinate pout. Simone found him waiting anyway, sitting on a plastic chair with his back to the house. The grass was ravaged by green plums and glistening with water. Claude sat swaddled in a blanket, his shaved head poking out, bent and unsteady. Isolated patches of persistent hair had grown back, forming the rough shapes of a jigsaw puzzle. It occurred to Simone that it was the memory of this unrecognizable man she would be left with.

He had turned around when he heard her and his right arm came out of the blanket, like a beggar putting out his hand. The veins were wasted by the poison of the injections and formed a dull red web of tiny sensitive filaments under his skin. It made it look as though his diseased blood was thinning to the surface of his body. Claude had never yet talked about it; maybe he had only just noticed. He ran his finger over the lines and said that, oddly, the burning sensation froze his limbs. His skin was poisoned and was recoiling in disgust. He could no longer bear warm water, he added, pulling down his sleeve.

The noise of a moped slaloming down the street drew his attention to the house. He stared up at the closed blinds of Gaël's room for a few moments, then glanced impatiently at his watch. His annoyance asked for no help. Simone knew he would bear the disappointment of feeling so little understanding and pleasure alone and without a word. She hoped for his sake that it was not just guilt complicated by irreparable self-reproach and anxieties that were making him suffer the steady deterioration he was tracking so minutely. His silences unnerved her, sapped her energy. She rested her hips against the back of his chair and laid a hand on his neck, saying that he ought just to go off alone, that she would take the boy with her to work.

Claude got up to go and fetch her a chair and a coffee. The grass needed mowing, he observed, coming back to sit down. Behind the barricade of plum trees, the blinding heat of the morning was rising; on their side, the rest of the neighborhood did not exist. Claude took little sips of his drink, holding his cup through the blanket. After a long silence, when Simone thought he was toying with going upstairs to wake Gaël, he said that he had a strong feeling of death in him.

His manner was so objective that Simone was spared the need to protest. Claude was coming back to her the way she could understand and love him. Suddenly, the thought of her future solitude struck her with fresh cruelty. She started to shake and pressed two fingers to the corners of her eyes to crush any wish to cry. Claude laid his cup on his knee, took her hand, and apologized, although she did not really know what for. For losing hope? For having loved her by default? Because he didn't even feel any desire anymore?

There was a chattering of blackbirds tearing themselves from the tangled depths of the bushes. It had been ages since they had last heard the little birds chirping in the forsythia. Either they had not survived or they had flown off. Simone had not paid attention; she had stopped going into the garden alone. It was a month since she had had any pleasures or time to herself. The sun began to rise over the trees and the sudden rattle of blinds being pulled up reminded them of the houses close by. Claude glanced at his watch again and stood up, taking off the blanket. I'll be back for lunch, he said, then seemed not to know how to take his leave. Simone noticed that a dribble of coffee was trickling down the cleft in his chin. The image was so wretched on his irritated face that she dared not point it out. He had turned around and was walking away, feeling the top of his head in disbelief, with his hand spread out like a jellyfish. His self-consciousness is gauche and so sad, she mused gently. In the calm of the chilly garden, pity for herself and for him revived a distant sense of love.

Simone had gone upstairs to change the sheets, when Gaël finally blundered sleepily out of his room, although the morning was well advanced. He was wearing short pants, like long swimming trunks, which had cut into his hip, leaving a red groove. Little pockets of cellulite trembled in the olive skin of his bare chest. He had the swellings of a girl's breasts, with fleshy nipples as pink and delicate as lips. Simone had started putting clean sheets on the bed and she straightened up, a pillowcase over her hands, to watch him. He took two wobbly steps, as though walking over a bed of thorns; then he caught sight of her, clapped his arms across his chest and retreated into his room. The door gave a controlled slam. The brusqueness of his reaction caught her in the face like boiling water. She spun around to the window with the thought that she would have to make up for the insult of this misunderstanding without Claude. A group of cyclists had just come into view with the clunk of changing gears. Simone momentarily let her attention wander to the spectacle of them slowly fanning out as they left the street. Her heart had calmed down but was heavy with defeat. As usual on a Sunday, she had to go and pick up the week's files from the dentists' office and set out the instruments for Monday. It had been agreed with Jovana that if necessary, she would take Gaël with her. But the prospect looked suddenly impossible.

He had just left the bedroom. Simone heard him lock himself in the bathroom. The silence in the house and in the street since the cyclists had gone by was total. The sky was radiant, and the sun nibbled at the windowsill, warming the scent of dusty varnish. Simone hurriedly finished covering the quilt and picked up the pile of sheets. She rolled up Claude's pajamas; they were damp with cold sweat, causing her an unpleasant surprise that was almost alive.

Gaël was still in the shower when she went back up to his room. She thought she could hear him babbling to himself. A sweet, spicy smell floated in the stuffy half-light—a smell of feet. The backpack lay tipped over on the floor, choking on a tight plug of clothes that Gaël must have tugged on too hard. Simone put up the blinds and opened the window. An armful of light raked the sheets draped over the piles of boxes. As she began to shake out the blanket, candy wrappings, a dissected pen, and a forlorn earplug tumbled out. She put them on the bedside table. Jovana presumably never made the beds, because when Gaël came back from the bathroom, he stood for a moment with his cheeks puffed out and his hands crossed flat on his head, not knowing how to react. His wet hair looked combed down with brilliantine. He had put on a bottle-green bathrobe, still creased from the packaging, which gave him the appearance of a little man. Jovana must have bought it for him specially. Simone loved her for having thought of preserving his dignity, or for having risen to its demands. She wondered how much negotiating had been necessary for him to agree to come, and whether he had partly wanted to anyway.

Don't you ever make your bed? she asked, in an artificial voice she hated herself for. Yes, sometimes, Gaël replied, squatting down on his heels beside the backpack, which he considered unenthusiastically. He had realized he was about to be asked to tidy his things; seeing him acquiesce so reluctantly threw her into a panic. She was sure there was nothing left of their understanding of that first day. Anxieties brimmed up at her own disappointment.

Will you be bored if you come to work with me this morning? She was talking to his rounded back as he fumbled in the bag with what looked like deliberate clumsiness. She was just about to add that Claude would not be back before mid-day, when he turned around. His face was lit up by a marvelous inky smile from chewing his pen. He asked her out of the blue if she had opened the present. Simone looked at him uncompre-hending, then was abashed. She had completely forgotten! Her reaction made him laugh and flop forward against the mattress. His body had a kind of affected limpness that, oddly, invited familiar-ity. Simone rumpled his wet hair, and he flinched as though she were tickling him. We'll go open the package, she suggested, catching hold of the hand he held out for her to help him up. His hand was moist and dimpled and offered no grip or reaction. In fact, he was making no effort and let her take his full weight, arching backward with his head tipped back, caterwauling in a rather silly way. Simone yanked him upright sharply, oddly hurt by his clowning. He got to his feet and pre-tended to stagger, still cackling artificially, but he would not meet her gaze and his eyes clouded with a sly hint of anger.

A police car drove slowly past the house in a ripple of blue and white through the thick lace of birch leaves. Simone told Gaël to hurry up and get dressed; then she picked up the candy wrappers and left the room. Their misunderstanding left a nagging awkwardness; neither of them was quite able to act normally yet. Simone went down a few stairs. There was no more sound from the bedroom and she could not help glancing up through the banister posts. She caught a glimpse of him from the side, hunched and crimson-faced, tugging endlessly at the cord of his bathrobe. He got angry so quickly; it struck her as an unfathomable violence.

Before going out, Claude had rinsed out his mug, upended the bread on top of an unwanted slice, and put back the gift in the center of the table, where the meticulous smears of a sponge were drying out. Simone tried to untie the knot, then cut the ribbon and set about unsticking the adhesive tape without tearing the paper. There was a silver key ring for Claude with a horse's head because that had been his sport when he was twenty, and for her, a chunky bangle also made of silver, though her name was missing because Gaël had not remembered what it was. A little card had been signed by the pair of them and said *Thank you* in a cloud of hearts. Simone sat down with the bracelet in her hand and felt inexplicably attacked, when suddenly she heard Gaël clattering down the stairs.

He came and sprawled his arms and chest across the table beside her. Do you like it? he asked with wonderful impatience before admitting honestly, when he saw how touched she was, that it had been his mother's idea. Now that his hair was nearly dry, it was bobbing messily again, making him look more childish. But Simone guessed there could be no question of kissing him. Their bare arms were so close on the table that the embarrassment between them was palpable. Still propped on his elbows, Gaël rocked back and forth, eyeing the place furtively. Simone could not stop looking at the perfect whites of his eyes under the long, dark lashes, the bee-sting purple of his lips, and that freshness and feverishness of youth that caused her a wave of nostalgia.

The breeze blew through the open house and raised the pages of a calendar hanging on the pantry door above an old photo of Claude and Cédric now spattered with splashes of grease. Gaël stared at it for a moment, looking greedy with secret questions. Then he flopped onto a stool and watched Simone put the gifts in a box. I didn't even think to ask what you have for breakfast, she said, apologizing. Gaël made a face in surprise. He ate crackers and a yogurt, but it didn't matter if she didn't have any. He was sweetly agreeable and his face was calmer; something approaching pleasure had returned, or a wish to feel she was happy. He had seen a little boy spying on them from under the blue curtain and wanted to know who he was. That's Malika, and she's a little girl, Simone corrected, although she could not be sure. She had never noticed the faintest movement behind the curtain. The idea that Gaël's presence was attracting attention in the neighborhood made her aware of their insecurity and the lack of protection Claude's illness had brought on them.

Gaël took ages finishing his milk and groping for his slippers under the table. Then Simone had to wait for him again while he went upstairs to put on his sneakers. Every move he made seemed dragged from the depths of a reverie that somehow slowly eased the sense of urgency to get out. Simone shouted to him from the hallway that she was about to leave. He caught up with her, panting and chattering, and insisted on carrying the bag with the folders in it and putting the empty trash can back in the garage. Just as they were finally leaving, the police car drove past the house for the second time. Gaël ran after it a few yards into the dazzling street. He had wrapped the handles of the bag around his wrist and it bounced against his leg, already a hindrance. His whole attention was again diverted from Simone. In fact, he was waiting for her to go on ahead, which she did.

When she turned around, he was standing outside the house opposite, peering through the hedge with his hands in his pockets, displaying the same attitude of awkward gallantry that had touched her the first day. She continued on a few paces, then stopped again to wait for him. The area was sunk in Sunday somnolence, every window open or the blinds down. Here and there, the wash swung from a line, and an inflatable wading pool lay wilting in the sun. Gaël was still messing around, trying to reach his hand into the hedge, twisting his mouth. His slack belly protruded under his T-shirt. He had put the bag down at his feet and almost forgot to pick it up when he finally bounded forward to join Simone.

The walk had bared his forehead, which was now mottled with red rings like fingerprints. Simone had only just realized that he had stopped where the cars must have gathered in the night. She wanted to know what he had found. Nothing, he admitted, disappointed, then added that he was sure he had seen one of the guys hiding something. He went on ahead of her, brushing so close to the fence that it caught his shoulder. What sort of thing? Simone asked. Her questions made him contemptuous. You know very well what it was, he trumpeted, stomping off noisily across the asphalt. Simone asked him to stop messing around. His ability to needle sometimes filled her with panic: she could not bear the thought of Claude's irritation. The image of his bald head surveying the street in the dusk left a bitter taste of pity. She blamed herself for letting him go to the stadium on his own, with his sickness on view like that. It struck her that he was moving and walking even more slowly. The treatment didn't seem to have slowed anything, helped anything; it had just added the lie to the uncertainty of waiting. It was impossible to get from him so much as an echo of his visits to the hospital, and Simone dared not call his doctor behind his back. And she had not yielded to the offer of one of the dentists, who thought she might be able to get hold of his medical file. Cheating like that would have been as good as condemning him to another death. But she desperately needed to know what would kill him and how and when, and especially whether Claude expected, like her, that one day he would feel he was suffocating.

They had arrived. Gaël had not said another word; he, too, seemed lost in his own thoughts and suddenly dejected, although he denied it, pursing his lips in a funny expression. The three dentists' offices were on the ground floor of a former apartment building surrounded by a fence and a messy strip of garden with untended bushes. Gaël entered the gloom of the hallway behind her. He thought it stank. His voice was quizzical again and set up a faint echo between the high ceilings and linoleum flooring of the shuttered rooms with their white-tinted windows.

Simone was only going to be an hour, and he passed the time rummaging around and leafing through the magazines but kept coming in to ask her what she was doing. She had never been in charge of a child before and was amazed how quickly she took on the constant distraction of a mother. The time comforted her. Gaël was not expecting to be looked after; he must be used to getting no reply to his questions and staying home alone, probably for whole evenings. It would have been tempting to ask him about his life, but Simone was afraid of giving herself away. The gifts plagued her with disturbing, insistent self-reproach. Claude had never paid Jovana any money. That had been the agreement, but it was so out of step with the situation. Simone wondered if Jovana had been hoping for something when she saw this sick man resurface in her life. Claude intended to acknowledge parenthood for Gaël and at least catch up on that, but Simone was sure Cédric would disapprove. She felt little compunction about judging him. Despite his extreme concern for them, Cédric never seemed to do things from the goodness of his heart. She saw Claude again as he had been the day before, after Jovana had left, his hand feeling the round hole in his bald scalp, the knotty veins of his feet in his new shoes. It was terribly painful to imagine how sorry he must be not to have had a more generous life.

The midday sun cast spangled slashes over the slate-colored linoleum. The heat was filtering through the shutters; the smell of ether was cloying. Gaël was both very pale and flushed. He kept coming in and hanging under the fountain at the sink in the office. A film of vapor glistened on his forehead. He wiped it off and pulled at the hem of his T-shirt, asking if he could go and play outside. A glimpse of his chubby belly revealed fine streaks of moisture beads. Again, Simone was struck by his cellulite bumps. She suddenly felt sure he must be diabetic.

Cédric's car was parked at an angle and sat half up on the sidewalk, right outside the garden gate. He must have gone to join Claude at the stadium and brought him back. He was biding his time out in the street and had apparently waited for them and even walked some of the way to meet them. A breeze had ruffled his hair and was blowing it back over an incipient bald spot, which Simone was surprised to see he was bothered about. He had one hand on his hip and was staring at something over the rooftops, as though to indicate to them that they need not hurry.

Gaël fell silent when he caught sight of him. Simone could not even hear the sound of his steps behind her. Cédric had not yet greeted them, or at least not openly. When she was almost at his side, he turned to her suddenly and straightened his shoulders. The shock of having seen his father bald and waxen was still written on his face. He was traumatized almost to the point of tears, she realized in astonishment as he came forward to kiss her. His cheek bulged with a lump of chewing gum and smelled of aftershave. He had put more weight on, and Simone suddenly knew that he had given up smoking. She had never imagined that his anguish and fear could be so irrational.

Gaël had stopped on the other side of the street and was kneeing the fence to bring down a great shower of seeds from the hedge, indulging an odd resentment by ignoring her and Cédric. You know we're kind of brothers, Cédric bantered, turning toward him with his arms folded. Gaël nodded with poor grace, stubbornly facing the hedge. Cédric was wearing a suede jacket and gray pants made of a nasty synthetic fabric. She thought he must look old to Gaël, from another world, or maybe the little boy sensed Cédric's perfectly controlled hostility. Simone went to ask Gaël to say hello, but he came forward of his own accord and held out a limp hand to shake. His lowered eyes seemed to be searching for a way out. The study window was open, and Simone suddenly realized what he had seen: Claude was on the phone. Cédric followed his gaze, too. That must be your mother, he confirmed, she called just as I was leaving. Cédric's attempt to get rid of him was thinly disguised. In answer, the little boy darted forward unexpectedly. He seemed about to leap over the gate but changed his mind, aware of his clumsiness and of other people's eyes on him. His gestures belied a kind of violence, a real rage against tears, which Simone suddenly realized she had seen him hiding since that morning behind sidelong glances.

Cédric waited for the child to turn up in the study, where Claude's silhouette cast a stooping shadow. It's totally weird seeing him like that, he blurted out, turning to Simone with a panicky smile. It took her a moment to realize that he was talking about Claude. She told him that his hair had fallen out in tufts and that he had shaved the rest off the day before, just before the child arrived. Cédric listened, jangling his keys in his pocket. His own vulnerability to his father's illness made him ill at ease and strung out. Simone would have liked him to comment on Gaël; she had a spiteful, pointless wish to see him drop the mask, a wish he had gauged perfectly well, because he would only agree that the resemblance was undeniable. But it was Claude who was bothering him, and it was not a distraction, but genuine shock. Simone could tell, just from seeing him so unhinged, how rapidly the sickness had progressed. It must be just as awful for a son as for a wife to see a man's dignity flake off in dead skin, diarrhea, and stale, scaly odors.

Gaël had replaced Claude on the other side of the open study window. Simone could see him twisting his cheek about on the receiver, bumping his hip against the desk, and fiddling with the pens in the metal goblet. His wriggling irritation depressed her. Everything about him had suggested grumpiness and defiance since that morning, apart from a brief moment of abstraction when cheerfulness had gotten the upper hand. But there was not much chance that he would ever really feel relaxed or at home here. Simone blamed herself for letting him be foisted on them and for having expected a bit of happiness. She just didn't have the energy to attend to anyone's suffering but her own.

Claude had wandered right, to the end of the garden. He had put on his invalid's tracksuit, and his bare neck stuck out of the top as though stretched by elastic bands. Cédric bent to watch him between the house wall and the birch tree's silver trunk. I managed to talk to his doctor yesterday, he announced almost absently, although that was clearly the whole reason he had come. The foci in the brain are stable, and the tumor in the lung has shrunk marginally, but not enough for them to operate, he added, still without looking at Simone and still as though it was incidental. Then at last he looked at her, took a deep, shuddering breath, and concluded that there was still hope that the treatment would keep him going, maybe even for another year.

His face was harried by bitter pain. Could

it be that he hated fate so much, that his filial loyalty had stayed so pure, despite the slights he had had to put up with? Simone felt herself blushing, surprised by her own feelings. She had wanted to believe that Claude was deteriorating; that was the truth of it. She could have started to yell, because the news had touched on the most shameful, most sensitive part of her. She felt as though her body had just registered, with sudden, treacherous force, the constant tension of seeing Claude turn into somebody else. She felt as if she were choking on cotton wool and revolt. Cédric had approached her and took her by the shoulder, shaking her gently to comfort her, but for what? His affection did not come naturally or easily to him, but Simone guessed he was moved to real sympathy. She said, I'm sorry, I'm stupid, then opened her mouth and took a slow, helpful breath, pausing before exhaling.

Claude was still at the bottom of the garden, as though arrested in his wandering by the wall of leaves that had taken years to hide them from the neighborhood. He stood stiffly looking up at the sky; then he let his head flop onto his breast and roll in an attitude of disbelief. What feelings of despair, what new desire to end it all had tempted him again? Simone was less and less able to bear witnessing his outbursts of regret. Cédric had moved away from her and was bouncing his keys in his hand. Yolande is waiting for me; I'm leaving, he announced, rubbing his face.

The car gave a little bleep, then a click as all the doors unlocked together. Cédric's face instantly hardened with worry of a different kind. Hey, come and look at this, he said, pointing to one of the wing mirrors, which was all but ripped off. That was done this morning, he declared with odd satisfaction. It wasn't yet midday and I was just coming into the parking lot.

For years, he had been trying to alert them to dangers that Claude refused so much as to comment on. Over the years, Claude had grown tense with disgust at these futile arguments, and it was impossible to know what his mute obstinacy meant, what it was trying to cure or prevent. Having been beaten up by one of his students had finally locked him into his opinions and silences. Simone guessed that the morning's incident must have revived the old arguments.

He now claims that he left the committee because of us. His tone was laconic, rebellious. He clearly wanted to see Simone finally come out on his side against Claude about the whole thing. She did not move, just raised her eyebrows in disbelief. It was all so long ago. She and Claude had been together for less than a year. He had been approached to run a kind of club for the local youth. It would have taken time out of the rare weekends spent with Cédric, and he had refused. He had probably not gotten over the regret and, after all these years, still blamed them and was making them pay for his choice. I don't believe he said that, she retorted calmly, relieved to resist the doubt. Cédric considered her reaction with a half smile that was both a sneer and an apology. Ask him. You'll see. That was his only comment as he came to kiss her. His hand lingered on her waist, like the smug apology of an insincere suitor. I shouldn't have told you, he said. It's legitimate to hate other people when you discover you're dying at fifty. Simone nodded, but her whole being recoiled. Cédric said good-bye, again unflappable and methodical. She watched him remove a leaf that was caught in the windshield, take off his jacket and fold it carefully on the passenger seat, then position himself at the wheel. His calm annoyed her; she felt an overwhelming urge to be alone.

Cédric backed off the pavement and stopped to take a last look at Claude, who was still at the bottom of the garden, his left hand dangling inert, as though dragged down by a lopsidedness he could not help. His arm doesn't seem to hurt him any more, he observed, imitating the way they had seen him shake out the pain all the time. Simone pursed her lips. Now it was the other arm that was burning on the inside; the sum of his torments was unchanged. Cédric nodded absently. His attention had wandered to the study window, which he indicated to Simone with raised eyebrows.

Gaël was perched on the windowsill and dropped heavily into a dark hole concealed by the bushes. He crouched down in a huddled ball for a few seconds as though on the alert, then sprang up and ran over to Claude, swinging his arms with childish, embarrassed enthusiasm. Maybe it was a spontaneous outburst, or perhaps it was suggested by Jovana, but when he reached Claude, he took his hand and leaned his head against his stomach.

Cédric wiped his sunglasses in the draft from the air conditioning. Looking through his sparse, fine hair, Simone could see beads of sweat glistening on the slight bald patch. There was no point trying to get him to say something; his frustrations always found consolation unaided. Simone bent down to the window to ask him to kiss Yolande and the little girl for her. He nodded *Okay*, smiled, and put up the window. Since the cancer was diagnosed, Simone thought wonderingly, he has always managed to summon up the requisite sympathy, even if it means he never gives vent to his feelings. She wondered why she found it so hard at least to acknowledge his untiring attachment.

Gaël had found things to do for the rest of the day. In the evening, after dinner, he wanted to play checkers with Claude. Simone was amazed to see him so focused. But it was mostly the pale skin of Claude's forearm freckled with brown marks that was intriguing him. The treatment was destroying his veins, she explained to him later. But Gaël knew that already. He had insisted Simone come and say good night to him, and he lay listening to her on his back with the sheet pulled up under his chin, looking a bit clownish. His eyes would not stay still under his bare forehead, where there was a little scratch that formed a row of dark beads of blood. He was prickling all over with impatience and curiosity, endlessly savoring questions, not all of which he asked. On the bedside table, a T-shirt, an electronic game, and the lone earplug lay in a heap. His sneakers were thrown down in a corner and gave off that sweetish, slightly spicy, slightly moldy smell that had surprised Simone when she was straightening his room. She sat down on the edge of the bed, and she could feel his legs moving through the sheet. His boisterous affection in this little man's inner sanctum intimidated her more than his silences and black moods. She wanted so badly to hug him to her that it hurt, and he must have sensed that perfectly well, because a provocative glint crept into his eyes. Can I tickle you? he asked with a big laugh, revealing gums sticky with chocolate. Are you eating on the sly? Her annoyance made him laugh. He sat up to seize her around the neck and draw her down to him. He wasn't tired and never went to bed this early, he claimed, simpering to stop her from leaving right away, or at least turning the light off.

In their absence, Claude had pulled the blinds down and switched on the news. The sound was turned down and the images, taken with a mobile phone, were almost indecipherable. Flames exploded and gesticulated in a crazy whirling hurricane, scattering powerfully agile, tiny hooded figures. Then the scene began to shudder to the rhythm of a breathless chase through the darkness of a deserted street. It had happened an hour earlier downtown, Claude commented without taking his eyes off the set. A young man had been killed during the night and now two police officers had been hurt. The flames were succeeded by a woman's face that seemed to have been pinned to the concrete wall of an apartment building by the midday sun.

Simone did not immediately recognize the place or, for that matter, the woman, who was one of the patients at the dentists' office. Her usually vindictive features were harried by a kind of nightmarish lassitude. She kept saying that it was a crime, not an accident, but oddly without anger, or else paralyzed by a presentiment of outbursts to come. Beside her, her eldest daughter pressed a handkerchief to eyes blackened by eyeliner. Her sobs gave her bright red lips an air of deep disgust. But it was she who foretold and condemned the current devastation, while the mother disappeared from the picture. Simone sat down gently on the edge of the sofa and thought, with a kind of dizzy feeling, that she had no way of sympathizing with these women whose son and brother had just been killed.

They're from around here, she said suddenly, as though asking for Claude's help. He gave a shrug of irritation and took a while to reply that he knew who they were. His agony was much more tangible and realistic: he had already paid for so much distress and revolt, and the outcome finally, two years earlier, had been an even harder abdication. His arms lay side by side on his thighs, one a bit numb from edema, the other wasted by chemotherapy. He had the horrified air of someone who found himself tied up. Simone had never felt such lack of sympathy for his feelings of guilt. She studied his profile in the flickering images and asked if it was really because of them that he had left the committee. His hollow cheek tensed briefly, as though grinding on bone and muscle. All I said was, you weren't interested in the problems of the neighborhood and my mistake was not to persevere. Simone thought he was going to add something, but he grabbed the remote control and turned up the volume. She hated the sickness for giving him the right to discredit in a sentence years of understanding that had been genuine and mutual.

The flames had engulfed the screen again. The picture was clearer. Jets of foam capered across it, and gradually, the gutted carcass of an upturned car straddling the street appeared underneath. The red smoke in the background made everything look strangely thick, as though the night had caught fire. Claude leaned forward to put down the remote control, when suddenly his head jerked up above the sofa. Simone just had time to make out Gaël's silhouette disappearing down the dark hallway. She glanced at Claude, as though he was now to be feared, then froze. His eyes were red; he was crying.

Why aren't you in bed? The question thundered out, but it did bring Gaël back to the doorway. He eyed Claude, half scared, half amused. He must see Claude's roughness and emotion as a kind of joke. I was thirsty, he said, oddly intrepid. Claude tried to get up, but his weakened leg gave way and he stumbled. You don't just help yourself without asking, he said in a voice that shook from the surprise of narrowly avoiding a fall. Gaël discreetly swallowed what he had had in his mouth. He had put on the green bathrobe over the T-shirt he had been wearing that day and the jogging pants he had on at dinner. Simone realized that he had been fully dressed under the sheets when she had gone up.

Claude had settled back in an awkward position, one knee folded under him and his arm flung over the back of the sofa. A tear he seemed not to know was there trickled down his chin; he caught it on the back of his hand with a startled look that must have shocked Gaël, who apologized and blushed but was nevertheless bold enough to approach the sofa, seeing that Claude's anger had been undermined. Since he'd come into the room, his eyes had missed nothing of what was happening on the screen. He asked if it was the district around here. His fascination was intense and transparent, and Simone suddenly saw what Claude was just realizing: that it was too late to teach him to hate violence.

THEY HAD STAYED UP late with the windows and shutters open, listening for the distant echo of sirens, standing silently side by side under a deep blue night sky, ruffled now and then by a flurry of pigeons. When Simone woke up, the street was intact and peaceful. A warm breeze was blowing heavy shadows of clouds across the foot of the bed. From the radio on the floor came the muffled announcement that the disturbances had died down shortly after midnight and that there was a risk of showers during the day. Claude had gone back to bed fully dressed and was lying on top of the sheets, his wasted, carefully soaped body furtively restless. Simone kept hearing him rustling in his pocket; it took her an age to find the strength to turn over to him.

He had plumped up the pillow under his head and was staring at her wide-eyed, as though hoping she would exonerate him for the self-reproaches he had been muttering for days. Simone laid her hands on his face to muzzle her own fears. She had the taste of dirt in her mouth and, above all, so little heart for sympathy—couldn't he see how badly she needed consolation herself?

Did you manage to get some sleep? she asked him, laying her hand on his shoulder. Even that simple contact caused him a brief shudder, for which he apologized, withdrawing his arm like a lump of dead wood. I spent the whole night worrying that Gaël would go out into it, he said angrily. Simone rolled onto her back and made no reply. There was nothing to say that would not have led to conflict. The next chemotherapy session this morning would make him even more uncomfortable than the previous ones. He had rubbed Nivea over his scalp and put on a salmon pink shirt to go there. Simone watched him sit down on the edge of the bed and put his slippers on with his clumsy hand. She envied him for not doubting his duties or his mistakes.

Claude was just about to leave when her brother called, clearly more curious than concerned about the previous day's riots. Simone told him that they had not seen anything, just heard sirens in the evening. Claude's preoccupied manner as he dawdled endlessly in the hallway prevented her from talking freely. He made her feel unfairly guilty for being unforgiving. Her brother's firm, pragmatic tone justified her sense of revolt. He was untroubled by tolerance or complexes when he said that there was no excuse for making a whole district pay for a death that had probably been an accident. And that was what Simone felt she had a right to hear after the fears they had suffered.

Why don't you come over for a change of scene for a few days when the child has gone, he said in an undertone, as though Claude might have heard. Simone cradled the receiver closer to her cheek and replied that she couldn't. The suggestion brought her not the slightest prospect of relief. With Claude, she had lost the habit and the need to confide in other people, including most of her friends, from whom she had grown apart since coming to live here. It was pointless while he was alive to think of taking a break from the torment that would have to be endured, day after day, out of loyalty to each other.

As she hung up in the kitchen, she saw a moped leaning against the open gate in the tall grass on the other side of the street. The owners were away and had sent someone to check that there had not been any damage during the night. The blinds of the French door to the garden were raised halfway; a young guy in a polo shirt and cream Bermuda shorts was scouring the environs from the upstairs balcony. Simone guessed from his air of annoyance that there was nothing to see, nothing to deplore. Witnessing other people's fears comforted her. It is so much more arrogant to think that you don't have to defend yourself, she thought, feeling a sudden urge to cry as she watched Claude leave the house.

Gaël must have been watching him go from his room, because almost immediately he appeared in the kitchen. He had not showered and was already dressed, and he wanted to know what she was looking at and who had called earlier on. His hair stood up in spikes and he flattened it down, first with one hand, then the other, trying to see the moped and the guy on the balcony. Simone could tell he was tempted to ask how long Claude would be gone. He was already playing subtle games with the liberties he could take in his father's absence and was watching her with his head tilted and one eye half-closed, waiting for her to guess and bend the rules about not watching daytime TV. But she pretended not to understand and, contrary to all expectation, he did not insist.

He wasn't hungry, but he let her press him to have a yogurt shake, which he drank while leaning one hip against the desk and whining that he was bored. The sky was clouding over, and the light cast yellow halos over the downy translucency of his skin. Simone found his whining and loafing, in the context of this day, particularly trying. The day before, he had helped Claude pick up the plums that had been driven into the lawn like nails. Simone suggested he give it another try, explaining that, in any case, it would take her only an hour or two to do the dentists' accounts. Gaël noisily emptied his puffed-out cheeks in disgust. His sour breath brought her upright with a jerk. He was clearly sick from eating too much chocolate in the night.

He turned to the trophies, his legs wrapped around one another and his belly protruding. His round hips raised two plump handfuls of flesh under his T-shirt. Simone took his hand to draw him toward her. You're not diabetic, are you? she asked, trying to make a joke of it and find out whether his mother had thought about taking him to see a doctor. He made a funny face at the word (or the liberty). Then, slowly, his face began to smolder. My mother doesn't care about you, he said, holding her gaze. His intention was unclear but so savage that almost immediately he had to run off.

Simone dared not move or breathe. She guessed that he, too, was on the alert in the living room. The wind had come up making it impossible to listen to his silence. Outside, the rotary washing line had begun to spin around in a great eddy of leaves, and she suddenly thought she saw a figure from the street running away. She stood up in a mad panic that felt like an explosion and called out, then opened the net curtains. Gaël made no reply: he had gone out into the garden. She saw him skulking around with his hands in his pockets, dislodging a plum with the toe of his sneaker and kicking it toward the basket. His heightened color had settled into big red blotches down his neck, like the marks from a garroting. Simone put her head out of the window but was again startled by a shadow: A long skein of crows sailed overhead and seemed to shatter among the branches. She sat down at her desk, chilly and trembling. Gradually, her terror dissolved into physical numbness and only the panicky thoughts it had brought on were left. She could not get yesterday's images out of her mind; they made her feel guilty, uneasy. She saw again the mother's horror and the daughter's disgust, and she went over and over their tragedy but could not get beyond a feeling of hostility. I'm not good, she thought, with a lucidity that was an almost comforting reaction to Claude's disenchantment and his accusations. But who is? And who in the area ever cared what happened to us?

When Simone next looked up from her computer, the first sparse drops of rain were casting long streaks against the windowpane.

Gaël was pinned to the fence, talking to Malika or her mother—Simone did not know which, as the forsythia screened them off. His familiarity filled her with a vague sense of insecurity. Nora, the mother, had remarried in the spring that Aude was born. Within just a few weeks, the new husband had had a willow cut down, although the tree's cascading branches had sheltered both their patios behind its swaying skirts. Suddenly exposed, they felt both spied on and nosy. No explanation had been given, none had been demanded, and Simone had just settled for not putting the table outside anymore. Since then, the hedges had thickened up and they had stopped noticing one another, but they had lost the habit of eating lunch in the garden. Simone had continued to exchange a few words over the fence with Nora, and occasionally she still dropped the little girl off at school. Then one day, just before Claude got sick, she had found the husband's son slumped in one of the deck chairs at the bottom of the garden, and there he had stayed till evening, an unmoving and worrying presence. Claude was out. Simone had gotten scared and called the father to come over and fetch him, creating a tension that still rankled.

Gaël was still chatting through the fence, bouncing his shoulder against it, ricocheting farther and farther back each time. Simone was inexplicably perturbed by his disobedience and inquisitiveness. She had the feeling he was going to come back and tell her things she didn't want to hear. But rain was starting to fall, straight down like a curtain, and Gaël was slowly coming through it with his arms outstretched, suddenly breaking into a run to get inside. Simone went back to her work, her body tingling with nerves exacerbated by lack of sleep and too much emotion. Several seconds crawled by before she heard the furtive scrape of a drawer in the kitchen, and he soon called out to know when they were going shopping. Simone turned around. He was watching her from the hall. His bangs clung to his forehead and were dripping water onto his smooth, untroubled face. He had lost a tooth, he blurted out, and came in to lay a rotten molar with a hole in it on the desk. His mouth was wide open and swimming in dark blood.

The mall was less than a quarter of an hour's walk away via the alleys of the old town, then along the side of the garden center. Gaël grumbled at the thought of having to walk, and Simone was easily persuaded to take the car, suddenly anxious at having promised to go out on a day like this. A thick ceiling of clouds scudded over the semideserted parking lot with its flutter of red bunting. Only a few shops along the walkway still had their grilles down. A man in a fluorescent jacket was piling up empty, rain-soaked crates beside some containers, and a guy in a tracksuit watched them park, stubbing out his cigarette on a tree trunk. Simone had not heard a squeak out of Gaël since they'd left. She could see his frowning face scanning the place intently. It was the burned-out cars that he had wanted to see, but she had refused, and anyway, she didn't really know where they would be.

Gaël was starting to be distracted out of his frustration. The metal shopping cart shuddered along to his humming. He marched down the aisles ahead of Simone, swinging his body and his arms, constantly coming back to suggest buying things that he ended up putting back more or less graciously. His face was twisted by the contortions of his tongue feeling around the hole where the tooth had been. He was still abnormally pale and his breath a bit warm and sour. The spiky tufts of the morning had reappeared in his hair, which he had combed down after the rain. Simone did not altogether recognize him and she found the idea oddly unnerving. A voice over the loudspeakers announced for the second time that the store would be closing early today, at six o'clock, and it was only then that she realized she was scared. Go choose what you want for lunch and we'll go home, she said, trying to catch sight of daylight.

Gaël beat her to the checkout, where she found him with a pack of ground beef clamped between his knees, playing with the bags of jelly beans that were hanging at one of the displays. He looked around for her with a smile on his face, exuding malicious defiance and arrogance, as though itching for her to see him shove one of the bags in his pocket. Intrigued, the checkout clerk raised herself slightly from her seat. There was a pirouette of exchanged glances, which he withstood for a few seconds with disagreeable temerity.

Simone caught up to him on the walkway in a whirl of drops as fat as beads. His cheeks were again mottled with bright red blotches, she noticed as she drew level with him. You didn't steal it? she asked as sharply as she could. Gaël seemed about to play the innocent, but sensing that she was really angry, he said it hardly cost anything anyway. His reasoning unsettled Simone's sternness momentarily. The memory of his brief angry outburst that morning lingered unpleasantly in her mind, creating a funny mix with the fears of the night and her present irritation. There was nothing left of her certainty about her affection and indulgence toward him. She was seized with sudden panic as she realized that she might no longer be able to put up with him and that she did not know what she had done with Jovana's number.

She plucked up courage to ask, Would your mother have let you steal them? It was a masochistic attempt to force him to betray his aggression again. But the question just baffled him. He thought it funny to make such a fuss about that. *That,* what do you mean by *that*? she asked, trying to get him to explain. The fat drops were buffeting them irritatingly. Gaël made a face and walked on. Simone's earnestness was becoming a drag. He quickened his pace, then broke into a run till he reached the car, slamming into it flat on his belly with an affected groan, which she ignored.

The lowering sky had turned yellow with a weird stir of patches of sunlight and circling seagulls. Simone hurriedly put the bags in the trunk, busying herself as a way of off-loading her agitation. Gaël squatted silently beside a wheel, pressing his fists determinedly into his cheeks. Simone called to him but did not wait to go and put back the shopping cart. When she came back, she found him standing by the car with an odd look about him.

A dozen yards behind him, two young guys were loping toward them between the cars, taking oddly synchronized steps. Simone unlocked the doors and Gaël shuffled onto the backseat without taking his eyes off her, as though anxious that she hadn't noticed anything. He slammed the door and froze into a huddled, awkward pose. A volley of hailstones clattered against the windshield as Simone struggled to put on her seat belt. She started the engine, failed to get the windshield wipers to move, and looked for Gaël in the rearview mirror. He ducked his head as he sensed the two shadows reach the windshield, cowering as their clothes brushed insistently along the side of car. Only after the figures had reappeared in the next row of cars did he suddenly seem bizarrely excited.

Delicate strings of hailstones like white icing tumbled down the grooves in the hood. On all sides, the cars blazed in the sunshine, then instantly faded again. Simone turned the wheel numbly. Blood pounded deafeningly in her ears. The two guys looked around, as though amazed she was taking so long to move. Their eyes in their impassive faces were fearless, though they could not have been more than fifteen; their bodies were slim and wiry, already experienced. Simone felt they were looking at her as a woman, a woman judged old and despised. She hated them as much as she hated herself for being in such a panic. Her chest rose with an asthmatic wheeze. The car was only half out of the parking place, but all her actions were so out of control that she had to stop. In the mirror, Gaël's expression clouded. What are you doing? Why don't you go? he muttered in embarrassment, stretching out against the seat back. Simone snorted a kind of little laugh when she realized that he was ashamed to be with her.

No more words passed between them throughout the return journey. Simone drove over a carpet of hailstones into a flaming burst of sunshine. Gaël hunkered down, tongue-tied, aware that disobedience had gone from his side to hers. As soon as they were home, he darted up to his room.

Simone was putting the last of the food in the fridge when he came back down. He had put on a dry T-shirt. His mood seemed to vacillate between gloom and chicanery. He went and parked himself by the sink, craning his neck toward the window and asking when Claude was coming home and whether his mother had left a message. Simone replied in a tone of easygoing weariness that she had no idea. Drizzle was scattering the leaves, and a pleasant smell of warm steam filled the downstairs rooms. She longed for peace and silence.

Gaël had taken off his sneakers, and his socks left damp little footprints on the tiles. Simone noticed a broad scar on his shinbone. She asked him if he had broken his leg, but she got nothing but a sulky shrug in reply. He leaned against the cupboard, its knob tucked between his shoulder blades. I know why Claude was crying yesterday, he said suddenly, looking down at his toes, which were waggling in his socks. Simone said, Oh yes, why was that? But she really wasn't paying attention, distracted as she was by nagging fear and rage.

Aren't you going to tell me why? she insisted as it dawned on her what she had heard, puzzled that he had fallen quiet. She came over to him and crouched down, trying to smile up into his face, but he stubbornly refused to look at her. Her teasing brought a giggle from him and a childish arm movement that made him turn right around. Pressing his forehead against the cupboard, he fought her off with his elbow, then began to stammer in a rather silly voice that Claude was crying because it reminded him of when he had let the girl's face get slashed.

Simone felt a strange rushing noise sweep

through her and numb her senses. So that was how things had been talked about in the neighborhood, she thought, almost glad that people were justifying her lack of sympathy. Even back then, that had been Claude's mistake: to think you could reason with people holding deep-rooted and obtuse grudges. Training sessions at the club had been poisoned for weeks by rivalry between several teenagers on the handball team. Claude had ended up shutting two of the girls in the locker room and had given them an hour to get their hearts and brains in gear and settle the thing like adults.

The girl was turned to the wall when he had opened the door; her face was buried in her T-shirt, which was dripping blood onto the floor. Simone had been called an hour later to the emergency room, where Claude was waiting, his neck and shoulders encased in plaster. I didn't know blood stank, he managed to say despite his anesthetized jaw, grabbing hold of her arm like a rope. He couldn't remember anything else, neither having seen that the girl's cheek had been all but sliced off and that she was holding it in place with her T-shirt, nor having been shoved out of the doorway by the second girl as she fled. At the trial, he was still in the neck brace, so he had to stand rigidly (arrogantly was what they said) under the merciless stare of the two families. Simone was left with a humiliated sense of his testy insistence in denying all accusations of having acted out of turn. His view was that his responsibility—everyone's responsibility—was not to protect violent behavior by showing the perpetrators leniency, but to force them to get a grip on themselves. He was sincere, indignant and unsmiling, obstinately resistant to the lure of hatred that the tragedy exposed him to. Yet his face was wedged in a roll of yellow foam, his cheeks squeezed almost comically. Simone had blamed herself for having thought he was a coward and then having found it difficult to love him, and for feeling nothing but rejection for the animosity he aroused.

Claude had never gotten over not having been vindicated. He said he had been betrayed, and he had grown bitter, had refused to discuss any of it again, and had lost interest in the community without agreeing to leave. Then he had wallowed in predictions about future guerillas but had refused to accept any responsibility or to excuse them. The pain in his back had appeared a few months later. He had put up with it for nearly a year before complaining. With hindsight, Simone had sided with Cédric in imagining that he had deliberately waited too long before seeing a doctor.

Simone must have looked funny, because Gaël tried to slither out of view. She caught his arm, conscious that she was pressing into the tickly hollow under his arm. You can tell Malika or her mother—I don't know whom you were talking to—that Claude just trusted that the two girls would be able to sort out their disagreement. Gaël nodded. His intimidated smile seemed to be trying to foil her sudden oddness. A wasp buzzing insistently around the window caught his attention. He gingerly wriggled free, ran over to the window, and nervously punched it closed, then stayed on tiptoe, intrigued by what was going on outside.

The ambulance had pulled up in front of the house. Claude slowly unfolded himself into the rain that was now falling gray and steady, his face looking small and crumpled in his outsize head. Gaël sank back on his heels and asked if he could go up to his room. He disappeared, sliding over the floor in his socks, then stopped dead in the doorway. It was Mom who told me about the girl, but ages ago, and maybe I didn't remember it right, he said with his back turned, before escaping up the stairs.

It took Simone a moment to register the significance: Claude had already gotten back in touch with Jovana during that period. The information stood out, jarring with the memory of their imprisonment back then and his rigid face trapped in the vise-like neck brace. Simone had gotten through those horrible weeks without showing any sign of how shaken she felt by the disaster. They had, in fact, treated each other with considerable care, forcing themselves to make love, sometimes with painful moments of real pleasure. But it was the memory of Jovana that had been uppermost, so much so that Claude had agreed to betray and pretend. Simone felt sorry for their relationship, a relationship of old people, she thought, tasting the bitter dregs of her pain. How far had Claude managed, at least at first, to believe that they would be able to comfort each other? She felt that she had badly screwed up both her chances and their relationship.

Claude gently closed the front door and gave the little cough that always announced his presence. When Simone did not see him appear, she went to the door to look into the hallway. His face took on a pained look as he caught sight of her. His salmon shirt clung to his bones; the dark circles of his nipples formed a kind of second expression of astonishment through the transparency of the wet fabric. He had gotten caught in the rain or had tried to relieve the nausea that still dazed his features. His clothes gave off a whiff of diarrhea, Simone realized, hearing the excruciating despair in his voice as he said that he would not be having any lunch. She stood smiling at him, incredulous and moved that it took so much humiliation to get the point of forgiveness. At least we'll have had these shared moments of self-deprecation, she thought. She told him that he could go upstairs, that the child was in his room. Claude waved his hand as though to make sure she kept out of his wake. The town is swarming with armed police, he said, sighing, as though that was what he had to atone for with his sufferings.

Simone had backed away to the sink, from where she could see the street through the fine threads of water dripping off the roof. The house opposite was shut up again and the rain had completely flattened the grass already bent from the gate passing over it. Claude had gone upstairs. Simone heard him slam the bathroom door, open the roof window, then turn on the shower, and soon after, she heard him start to cough up the bile he would be vomiting all night. This now-familiar collapse left her powerless and somehow vacant and slowed down. She went out into the hallway, where the warmth of recent days had gathered, and moved to the foot of the stairs, sliding her shoulder along the wall. Gaël was up there, with his arms dangling over the banister, his resting head a mass of tousled spikes. He straightened up when he saw her and gave her a sucked-in smile that seemed to beg her permission to come downstairs.

His clammy palm stuck to the glossy finish on the handrail. He stopped from stair to stair to listen to the sobbing with which Claude exhausted his nausea. Mom told me that would happen, he said straight out, as though telling Simone she need not feel guilty. His capacity for compassion, both contrite and mature, was wonderful. Simone put her hand around his neck and gave him a gentle shake, trying not to give way to tears. Shall we see what's on television, she asked, letting him go. The suggestion threw him into an extraordinarily turbulent indecision. Simone smiled, blew her nose, and said, Today, everyone can do as they like.

Gaël had run to jump onto the sofa, where he squeezed himself sideways in among the cushions. Simone came and sat down next to him for a moment. His feet in their socks were a bit repugnant; he slid them under her thighs and wriggled them about. He took a kind of affectionate aggression in needling her, and for the first time, Simone realized the nostalgia they would have to put up with when he was gone. She stood up so as not to grow weepy and went to shut the door to the garden. It was cool and bleak; no ray of summer pierced the now-persistent rain. Simone closed the French window. The damp was keeping them indoors. Gaël gathered up a throw and buried himself in it, as though trying to stay out of the way.

Simone went upstairs to ask after Claude, whose steps had creaked overhead several times already. She found him lowering the rolling blinds in their bedroom. He turned to her with hollow eyes, startled at the sight of her. He was completely incapable of all pretense. Simone hoped he would at least be loving enough to smile or apologize, but nothing. I'll leave you, then, she said, closing the door. She felt so despondent that she toyed for a few seconds with the brief hope that she might manage to tell him that she couldn't bear it anymore and was leaving.

She had lunch alone with Gaël in front of the television, and she left him there when she went back to work in her study. The leaves nodded gently in the rain, numbing her thoughts whenever she lifted her head from the computer. She wanted some chocolate, wanted to make herself feel sick. Every now and then, Gaël's revelations returned to the pit of her stomach with a shock that caught her breath unpleasantly, although the sensation didn't last. From the living room came the monotonous echo of lisping voices and springy sounds. Claude had not made a sound for several hours by the time Cédric called.

He had come home from the office early and wanted to know how Claude was coping with the new chemo. Simone told him about his repeated vomiting and the comatose silence that had followed, but she said nothing about the smell of diarrhea. Talking about it helped and reassured her about what she could still lucidly put up with. Cédric said he would try to stop over on the weekend. He made no comment about the riots, as though he thought they were both a bit to blame. Simone was glad she did not have to hear him flare up so unsympathetically, reminding her uncomfortably of her own feelings. Claude had always been a watchdog against prejudices she had held when she came to live here, and she had grown bitter burying and concealing them, she realized now, studying the reflection of the strained lines down her face.

Her sandal had slipped off under the desk. As she pushed back her chair to feel for it with her foot, she saw that Gaël was standing there, listening to her, peeping around the half-open door. He looked tired, dazed by images. His face was damp and burning from the warmth of the throw. Mom still hasn't called, he whined when Simone had hung up with Cédric. He was idly fanning himself with the door; then he asked if he could maybe make a call. Simone had not managed to find the number, but he knew what it was. He pressed the buttons down with great concentration and took a deep breath as he listened to the rings (like an agitated lover, Simone thought to herself) and came up with Jovana's voice mail. He left a short, courageous message. His dejection hung in the room. Claude still did not move upstairs. Outside, rain fell relentlessly on the distant summer-evening scene: a long, brilliant white line, with the trees silhouetted in the foreground. It's going to be a nice day again tomorrow, Simone said, to console him as much as herself. I'll get some work done and we'll find something fun to do.

It would soon be time for dinner and bed. Gaël whined ill-humoredly at the idea of having to take a bath. Simone could not face anything anymore, least of all getting him to obey. She told him she just wanted silence. Gaël nodded his head gravely and edged backward through the half-open door. The tinted glow from the computer screen in the darkening room flickered on his disappearing profile. Simone blew him a kiss and tried not to give way to too much emotion or scruples. He had almost shut the door completely, when, through the thin glimmer, Simone heard him ask whether he could go home soon.

SIMONE HAD NOT shut the door to the garden. The first brittle light of day after the storm dragged her from sleep. The grass still needed mowing and was a bright, spongy green, with a splash of color from a plastic bag that had blown in from the street. Simone turned back the throw and piled up the cushions under her head. Having slept and awakened without concern over Claude's suffering brought her a strange sense of anxious respite. They had never spent an impulsive night here with all the windows open to the garden. How far would Claude have let himself be happy in another life? Simone could not even picture him letting go. She felt almost more embarrassed than hurt at the thought of how troubled he must have been to discover pleasure with twenty-year-old Jovana. The bold, seductive generosity of that woman made her feel she had no excuse for regrets she could never make up for. I was so miserly with my love, she told herself, remembering that Gaël had asked to leave.

It was still extremely early. Sleep weighed her down but did not take over. She put the television on, then turned it off. The night had been calm; at least they had not had the wail of sirens echoing around them beyond the still darkness. The unease of the riots already seemed a thing of the past, and Gaël's moodiness was the only lingering worry. Simone sat up and rubbed her bare white legs where stubbly hairs had grown back. Not having to be there for other people brought her one of the few pleasures she really craved. She opened the door, made herself a coffee, and went out barefoot over the water-glazed grass. It was going to be fine; there was something curiously unbridled about the garden after the storm. The plums left on the trees were starting to acquire the plump purple flesh of ripe fruit. Simone pulled down a branch to pick one. The sour skin resisted, then yielded, and she found her mouth full of a revolting gritty mass of wormy tunnels.

There was no sound upstairs; it was all shut up and dark. Simone went up to take a warm shower, which brought forth from her a soft moan of stress finding release. When she came out, the radio was murmuring in the bedroom. Claude was awake. He lay curled up, a bulky shape in the gloom, which was broken by a just few streaks of light. The muggy atmosphere and smell of ether were suffocating. But Simone dared not open the blinds. Claude's silence met her like a wall and lasted several seconds. Then he groped for the knob on the radio alarm and everything in him seemed to brace itself as he turned over with a comatose writhe.

You slept downstairs. It was a bald statement of fact, which Simone felt she had to justify. You were so bad, I didn't want to be in the way. She took a step forward, but he shrank away from her with the slow contraction of a swatted insect about to die. Don't come in; I stink. His voice sounded sticky with saliva. He was about to add something, but the sentence broke off in a spasm that threw him out of the sheets. His huddled figure listed slightly to his weakened side. Simone moved aside to let him pass. The bathroom door gave a faint creak as it opened, and she saw him bent and trembling with all his might as he heaved and voided the bile that turned his stomach again and again.

The garbage truck was passing down below in a clatter of plastic containers and the sigh of exhaust. Simone remembered that she had not put out their garbage, that it would be too late to mow the lawn, and that countless chores were piling up without being attended to. Claude had flushed the toilet and was rinsing out his mouth. He went back into the bedroom without appearing to see her, crawling desperately slowly into the sheets and arching his arms over his face and head, as though begging her to leave him alone. Simone waited a while before she withdrew, but he called out to her. You should be careful not to put perfume on. The slightest smell upset him, made him feel sick. Simone knew this and had only put cream on her face. Claude's autocratic irritation seemed so incongruous and ruthless. She closed her eyes for a long moment before managing to say in an almost neutral voice that she was very sorry.

Vexation had revived the surprise of yesterday's revelations and brought her a kind of sudden sense of freedom. She decided to spend the day at Yolande's with Gaël. The prospect of just taking a few hours off from the sickness seemed like her greatest pleasure for months. She tapped at Gaël's door and was amazed by his instant, alert *Yes.* He would be with her in a minute, he added loudly, as though shouting to her not to come in.

Yolande took a while to answer. She had just come in from the garden and her breathless hello was bubbling over with joy. Simone never called in the daytime; in fact, she never called Yolande at all. She was surprised to hear Yolande and picture her in her domestic life, guessing that she must have decided on it herself, like a free pleasure that she would answer for. Cédric sometimes came over to see them, but they had never paid a return visit, not since Claude had started treatment. Simone was longing for the wonders of the hundred-year-old garden in summertime, where rosebushes nodded their heavy heads against the brick walls, red fruit grew in profusion, and the mulberry tree cast dense shade over a little path, staining the gravel such a dark blue with its berries, it was almost black. Yolande suggested they have lunch at home and go to the swimming pool afterward. She asked nothing about Claude, fully suspecting that this visit was an escape. Her tact and complicity were so unexpected that Simone unraveled. She confided (at the same time as she discovered) that she couldn't take it anymore. Yolande did not answer right away, as though to give Simone's confession its full weight. Aude was playing with a squeaky toy at her feet; she picked her up and said, Come over now to give yourself time. Simone was grateful she didn't add anything. She hung up and stood motionless for a long time, thinking over the years she had let pass before the immutable sight of the forsythia fanning out against her window.

She was on her way to get a cup of coffee a little later, when she found Gaël in the living room, parked in front of the television, his long T-shirt pulled on back to front and a yogurt drink in his hand. He looked a bit disheveled, slumped in a state of semiundress that contrasted with the avidity with which he was guzzling the images on the screen. Simone was perturbed not to have heard him thumping down the stairs or helping himself from the fridge. He hadn't heard her, either, and he blushed crimson when he turned around, swiftly putting down the yogurt and grabbing the remote control, but Simone was quicker.

We eat breakfast in the kitchen, she scolded, switching off the TV. Gaël flung himself on his back on the sofa. He pulled his T-shirt up over his head and lay there for a moment with his face hidden. When he peeped out, he wore a different expression: amused and stubborn, as disarming as his rebuff the day before. He stared at her, his fingers fiddling languorously with the deep folds of his belly button. He seemed totally unabashed, either about his body or his insolence, and this new behavior touched an inexplicably sensitive spot in Simone. She grabbed his arm to tell him to go upstairs and get dressed. We're going to the swimming pool near where Yolande lives, she went on, forcing down a rising wave of panic. You're going to meet your niece. Did you know you have a niece? The information intrigued him but put him on his guard. He sat up on the edge of the sofa and asked who she was and what her name was. But his voice sounded insincere and somehow uncaring.

A sudden gust of wind flung a shower of rain right onto the patio and scattered little disks of sunlight all around the room. Gaël flopped onto the sofa again and shielded his eyes with his arm. He pretended to yawn, and when he heard that they were expected at Yolande's for lunch, he began to knee the cushions about. Simone felt she was losing ground. The thought that he was hoping to stay and watch TV was like an assault. You're surely not stupid enough to waste your life in front of the television was her parting shot as she left the room. The retort he flung at her was said in too much of a mumble for her to make it out. She went back to the office, calmly closed the door behind her, and sat down with her chin on her folded hands, then sought and found where she had put Jovana's number. There was something like a lover's bitterness in her eagerness to send him home. Perplexed, she realized how badly she lacked and yearned for affection she could freely embrace.

Gaël eventually went up to his room, dragging his feet like a pledge of ruefulness. Simone felt irresponsible for revealing how fragile she was. A former colleague had left a message the previous day. She listened to it again as she finished her coffee. She ought to have returned the call, but she could not bring herself to describe for the umpteenth time since the start the concatenation of sufferings; talking about them rang false in her own ears. She was aware of never giving anything that might help people offer useful sympathy. Such conversations forced a mutual effort that was frustrating and militated against friendship. It's not the day to inflict that, she decided as she switched off the computer. Gaël was still not ready, and Simone had heard nothing more from him. She went up a few stairs to call to him in an undertone to hurry up, that it was nearly ten o'clock. Her own anger had completely subsided and she knew that his would not last. The pleasure of escaping for a day was bound to return.

The throw was still in a heap on the floor and, the cushions were scattered about, and the yogurt bottle had toppled off the coffee table. Simone briefly took stock of the chaos that was setting in behind Claude's back. The TV was still on, she noticed suddenly, seeing a rectangle of images shifting on the windowpanes. She felt about for the remote control in the sofa, flicked mechanically through the channels, and sensed suddenly that Gaël was nowhere in the house. A wave of heat broke slowly over her. She ran upstairs and was again struck by the smell and the muggy atmosphere. Gaël's bedroom door was ajar. A tepid bundle of sheets had been pushed to the foot of the bed and bunched-up clothes filled the half-light. He was not in the bathroom or in the kitchen, and she went out to look in the garden, already knowing he would not be there, either.

The basket of plums had vanished. Simone found it under the forsythia, tipped over the pile of rotting fruit. Someone had ripped branches off the hedge, stripped off the leaves, then stuck them like javelins into an exposed corner of fence where there was a gap in the hedge. The bottom of the mesh had been twisted up, leaving a small hole just big enough for a cat to get through but not a child. It was an act of silly but intentional vandalism, which Simone had not seen when she got up, the signs of a fit of rage she could not place in time and which sent shock waves through her.

It was starting to grow heavy; warm steam from the rain was rising off the sunny lawn. Simone went over to the house again then out onto the sidewalk, where she looked up and down the deserted street, which was still drenched in pools of light. The realization that he had run away filled her with a kind of exasperation of tiredness and guilt. She did not know how to break such senseless news to Claude. She was a bit inclined to tell Yolande instead, but in the end she went upstairs.

Claude must have been drifting off again, because he turned to her with an expression of pain and disbelief. Gaël has gone, she told him, and was instantly sorry she had come upstairs. It took him a few moments to react and prop himself on an elbow. The news did not surprise him; rather, it seemed to confirm him in his remorse. Have you gone to look at Nora's, he asked, sitting up on the edge of his bed. His mouth was set in such nauseous disgust that Simone berated herself for inflicting this on him. But he stood up, balancing himself carefully on both feet. He put his bad hand to his head, tremblingly, then fumbled with the neck of his pajama top and found that it stank of vomit. Simone thought it was pointless dumping such trouble on a person.

All seemed quiet next door when Simone went to ring the bell. It was Malika who opened the door. She was wearing a bathing suit under a great scarf that billowed around her like a cape when she ran to get her mother. Simone had gone there only two or three times in ten years. In the room off the hallway, dust particles hovered in the sun filtering through the net curtains. Simone noticed deep armchairs with cushions all askew and a jigsaw puzzle that someone had started on the carpet. Malika came back and leaned against the door frame in front of her, saying that her mother was coming. The bangs plastered across her broad forehead gave her an adult, slightly disapproving expression. Traces of sparkly polish edged the nails of her long brown feet and a thick gilt bangle clasped her arm above the elbow. She had a graceful figure, with shapely muscles and bones. She's not a little girl any longer, Simone realized, thinking how she had often driven her to school without any bond developing. You never come around to see us anymore, she said with false enthusiasm, and got no reply.

There was a rattle of windowpanes as a door slammed, and Nora appeared at the end of the hallway, from where she asked what was going on. She leaned one elbow up against the wall, and under her long camisole, the slack outline of her free, naked breasts was obvious. Neither she nor Malika had seen Gaël since the previous day. Simone did not feel at liberty to say that she was really worried. Having Nora standing there, exposed and distant, seemed to her the most unfriendly thing she had had to put up with in a long while. She said, *Okay*, apologized, and closed the door behind her. Until she was back on the street, she had the crazy feeling she might be shot at from behind.

It was past ten o'clock. The few neighbors who were not away on vacation must have been out. The street stretched white and quiet under the dull veil of steam rising off the puddles. Simone took a few hurried steps, then slowed down, embarrassed by the echo she set off all around her on the street. Behind a metal gate, a man in a bathrobe was raking up leaves that the night-time rain had shaken from the trees. Simone asked him about Gaël. She felt she was aping someone more concerned than she was. The man shot her a look, as though the question was an insult, then replied that he hadn't seen anyone. Simone turned back, at a loss. Nora was waving to her from her doorstep: she had put on a linen blouse and loose pants that had a fake, tattered elegance. I don't think he'll come to much harm with all those cops around just now, she called out, looking Simone up and down as if she were a waif who needed help. Reticent as it was, her sympathy was nevertheless some comfort. Simone blamed herself for being vulnerable and distrustful. She indicated that she was going back indoors and said they would go and look for the child in the car.

Claude was dressed and had come downstairs to wait in the hallway. Simone saw him sliding across the floor toward her to avoid the jolts that might still arouse his nausea. He had not taken a shower and the skin on his face was floury with dry patches that made him look a mess. Everything repulses him and makes him feel sick, thought Simone, but she was grateful that he was taking things in hand. He suggested she stay home while he searched the local streets in the car, and he took down the keys from the board in the hall and went out, squeezing her hand. This awkward, trusting grasp, such as he had not given her since their early days, caused in her a wave of tenderness, nostalgia, and apprehension. With tears in her eyes, she watched him as he walked away, taking desperately careful steps. She had never seen him look so fragile, so much like the walking dead. She reproached herself for letting him go but felt she was not the right person to go looking for a child of eleven. In reality, she was not even able to assess correctly how worried she was.

Silence returned, plunging her into a kind of lethargy. She went from her study to the living room, then back to the kitchen, where she drifted into a trance, gazing out at the street. Nora was at the garage door when Claude backed out. She gave a little tap on the hood for him to put down his window. It seemed to Simone that the hard streak in her was shaken by the surprise of seeing close-up the tragedy of this pale waxwork. Claude cut the engine and clung to the edge of the window, as though afraid of being jolted. Nora did not seem to notice this unfortunate instinct. As she talked, her folded arms rose in time to an agitation that had no thought either for Claude or for the situation. Simone went out onto the doorstep with the vague intention of intervening. Hearing her open the door, Nora spun around, a handful of keys raised in front of an unfathomable smile. Claude had started the engine again and slowly drove out onto the street. Nora looked after the car, then turned again to ask if she could come in. Simone saw her put her arm over the garden gate to pull up the latch; she had the unpleasant feeling that Nora was used to letting herself in.

Nora kicked her sandals off in the hallway, placidly observing that Claude didn't look at all good. Simone did not like seeing her walking barefoot through their house when their old grievances had never been cleared up. She offered a few factual explanations about Claude's treatment but knew she could not possibly confide in her. Nora had never been beyond the hall. It's funny seeing the house from here, she said, going out onto the patio. She walked under the shadow of the branches, stroking the lawn with her foot, and picked a plum but found it sour and seemed not to know where to spit it out. Simone watched her from the living room. Her nonchalance seemed insistent, affected. She wished she could have told Nora to go away; it hurt her to think of her finding the upturned basket and the torn-off branches, as if Gaël's violence was an indictment.

Did you look to see if he'd taken any money? Nora asked, coming back into the sitting room. Simone was so obsessed by her indefinable hostility that she did not immediately understand what she was talking about. Nora stared at her, impatient for an answer. Do you want me to go out in the car and look for him, too? The suggestion was serious but not insistent. Simone was convinced she was seeking to do just enough to retain the right to resent them, but for what? You know it's all over with Claude, she said as calmly as she could, yet desperate to break through her icy indifference. Nora countered this with words of reassurance that were neither heartfelt nor warm, so Simone repeated a bit more firmly that Claude was dying. It was the first time the words had been uttered out loud and it unhinged her. All deaths are terrible, she added, suddenly thinking she guessed why they had been judged.

Nora had heard Malika calling from the fence and turned around. Her long, aquiline profile twitched with displeasure. She did not actually understand Simone's attitude. The news about Claude's condition seemed to unsettle her, but it caused her no emotion. She said that she hadn't known and was sorry; then she added, after a long pause, that this was no excuse for having kicked her stepson out of the club.

Simone slowly interpreted the information, wondering if she should deduce from it that the willow had been taken down as a reprisal. A whole slice of her life here suddenly took on an unsuspected meaning. She again saw the teenager slouched for an entire afternoon in their deck chair; the strange threat of his unexplained presence in their garden was still with her. It was starting to grow warm. Nora shook her hair loose, letting it fall down her back. A drop of sweat trickled down the lines of her neck into the veiny hollow of her bare armpit. Simone realized, suddenly shaken out of her anger, that Nora must, in fact, be older than she was. A misgiving was gradually gaining ground, undermining her, rekindling old traumas; it seemed to her quite possible that the young man who had been killed two days earlier had also been expelled from the club by Claude. She asked Nora, but she gaped in wide-eyed perplexity. What should I know about it? she said, tying her hair back up. The question seemed to go on niggling at her, eliciting her incredulity, because she added with a ghost of a smile, I really don't think Claude was directly involved in what's happening. Simone took a step back, as though Nora's condescension had brushed up against her. Then what were you blaming him for just now? Nora took a moment before retorting with a dreadful shrug of her shoulders and saying she was annoyed, not for the first time, that he had sided with the cops. Her voice was curt again, assertive. Simone hated her for being wrong about Claude's intransigence with such conviction. He's dying after a short, demanding life, and all he managed to do was come unstuck, she thought calmly. Nora was probably interpreting the bitterness her face betrayed, because she declared ironically that they should just call her if they needed her. Simone followed her into the hallway. The slow sway of Nora's prominent shoulder blades under the light linen kindled an almost physical rage in her. Claude must have left the bedroom door open; the sick, cloying smell was gradually contaminating the corridor. Simone wished Nora would stay and see what this silent end nobody knew about was really like.

It took her several minutes to dispel the disturbing sensation of the visit and return to her anxiety. The morning was wearing on and with it the heat, made palpable by the buzzing of insects infesting the bushes. Simone went back to the fence to take another look at the remains of crushed plums being coveted by a swarm of wasps. The few snapped-off branches were wilting in the plastic-coated wire mesh. Simone was suddenly no longer sure she should see it as an act of rebellion. Malika was spying on her from behind the large waxy leaves of a bush that shaded a hammock. Her colorful silhouette came and went for a few seconds, then vanished in a flutter of scarf. Simone went back inside, wondering how she would pull herself together to get through the day. She had begun to straighten the sofa cushions when Yolande called, anxious that they had not yet arrived. She drove over in less than half an hour.

Simone saw her come through the garden gate and gaze around with an almost childish expression of empathy. Aude was dozing against her neck in a heavy white bundle. I told Cédric, she said as she kissed Simone. Her insistent smile seemed to inquire about the state she would find Claude in. Discovering that he had gone off in the car gave Yolande a shock, for which she apologized, but she accepted the information without judgment. She had not come back here since the cancer was announced, and Simone could see she felt guilty.

Aude woke up, blinking her eyes, her face tangled in the flyaway hair of her mother's chignon. A mosquito bite held one of her eyelids closed. Simone noticed but did not say anything. She was completely incapable of displays of affection, but Yolande seemed neither surprised nor shocked by this. She put the child on the ground, sent her off gently into the sitting room, and stood up, pushing back the hair from her forehead with a graceful gesture. Simone waited until Aude had disappeared, then crushed a feeble cry between her hands. Yolande gathered her in her bare arms. They were the arms of a very young woman and offered an awkward, intimidating refuge. Simone discovered that Yolande had a daughter's solicitude, which she did not know how to receive. She smells of lime blossom, she thought, freeing herself to wipe her nose and offer Yolande something to drink.

Yolande proved helpful, serene, and controlled. Her extreme thoughtfulness disarmed

Simone's defenses, and also her ability to react. Like Nora earlier, she asked if Gaël had taken any money. The question was pragmatic, with no hidden agenda. Simone was surprised to find that Yolande did not share Cédric's suspicions and opinions, although she was such a conventional, loyal wife. She was touched by her sexiness; she had a lithe, no-nonsense body, one that must be disturbing in climax. It was odd to imagine how someone as dreary and hidebound as Cédric had managed, at twenty-two, to win himself such happiness. Simone had never managed to get over her prejudice against the couple. She was annoyed with herself for having missed out on a potential friendship during all these years.

Claude came home just as Yolande was about to feed the little girl. She froze, as though scared by his ravaged head and obvious displeasure at finding her there. Her delicate skin grew mottled, and she made as if to gather up her daughter, a brisk reaction that Claude paid no attention to. I didn't find Gaël, but I left his description here and there, he declared, as though to preempt their rebukes. It was said with the same abruptness Simone had put up with back when he was heading, shut off and hurried, toward his death. She realized how much the treatment had subdued him in recent weeks, and, above all, how much it must have smothered his panic. Claude backed into the corridor and beckoned to her. I was sick in the car. I cleaned it up as best I could. I've got to go and change. The words were uttered with enormous self-disgust. He did not say (and probably did not want to admit) that he had not been in a fit state to look for Gaël properly. Simone watched him as he went upstairs, hauling himself up by the handrail, his back protruding through his shirt. She wondered what could be worse for him than being incapacitated in these circumstances.

Aude had tripped and banged her head against the window and she had begun to yell by the time he came downstairs. He sat down out of the way and glared at Simone, as though to fathom why she was inflicting their presence on him. He was back in his old jogging pants, which gaped over a triangle of pale skin as translucent as plastic. In the bluish light coming through the fabric of the lowered blinds, Simone did not recognize him. His eyebrows had fallen out completely, she realized after a time, and now his skull bulged under the papery skin and his dull, lashless eyes stared out at her. Like a mummy's head, she thought, smiling sadly at him. A dry patch was stuck to the side of his chin where there was no feeling, the side where his features were gradually growing numb. Simone hoped calmly that this meant the paralysis was finally taking a turn for the worse.

Claude leaned forward to turn on the television and the sound exploded into the room. He turned down the volume and flicked through the channels until he found what he was looking for: the same crazy, seething images of demonic flames and bodies, but reflected now in the glistening asphalt from the previous day's rain, and they had moved closer to home, so far as Simone could judge from the places she recognized. She thought back on her secret night beside the dark depths of the garden, and she felt as though she had been caught off guard by these fresh, unsuspected assaults in the community. I won't stay in the area, there's nothing I can solve and put right here, and there's nothing I want to do that hasn't been done for me, she promised herself, huddling into the sofa, and pressing her fingers into her burning eyes.

On a note of reproach and as though speaking to Yolande, Claude described how he had found most of the streets blocked off and empty of parked cars. He had not even managed to get close to the apartment buildings, where the inhabitants had taken up their positions in little groups and were angrily eyeing one another. He would not stop switching channels, then coming back to the night's stories, as though he might have spotted Gaël. Simone eventually opened her eyes to look at what was happening and then was sorry not to have remained ignorant. Dozens of youths were lunging forward, taking turns hurling fireballs at lines of cars and men barricaded behind Plexiglas. Claude had fallen silent. The scene satisfied an old pessimism that he could not forgive himself for having ceased to obey. Finding that Yolande had gone out into the garden to shield her daughter from it, he felt moved to make a pointlessly hurtful remark. Simone felt like screaming. She asked him to switch it off, but he did not hear and turned to her with that guilty look that exasperated her and made her feel depressingly powerless.

The afternoon dragged on interminably, slowed down even more by Aude's nap, which added silence to the hiatus. Simone could not settle her sense of panic. She couldn't imagine where Gaël could have gotten to, to go unnoticed for so long, and she was still upset at the thought that he was angry with them. Claude made a point of sitting with them, constantly at the mercy of rising vomit, which he held back by pinching his lips together. At last, he went upstairs when he heard that Cédric was about to join them. Simone had not dared to offend him by checking whether he had really looked everywhere and alerted everyone. She could not help thinking that they were becoming unforgivable.

Cédric arrived from out of town. It had been hot in the car and his shirt had lost its freshness and had ridden up out of his pants; he did not stop putting his hand up to his straggling hair over the beginnings of his bald patch. He smiled joylessly, wearily when he heard that Claude had gone upstairs without waiting for him. On his way over, he had stopped off at the accident and emergency unit, the police station, and the shopping mall. Simone was amazed he said nothing about the empty streets and loitering police vans. She sensed that he was annoyed and suspicious but unsympathetic, and she thought she noticed a kind of masculine aloofness because he knew he was beyond reproach. He had been with them nearly an hour when Jovana telephoned. Simone did not immediately understand why she was calling. Surprise left her speechless and crushed by guilt; it took a few seconds to concentrate on what she was hearing.

Gaël had gotten into a subway train, thinking he could find the apartment of one of Jovana's former boyfriends whom they often used to visit at one time, and he had lost his way. The security people at the station had contacted her because Gaël had not known Claude's number. Jovana dictated the details of the person to call to say when and where to pick him up. Simone was perturbed to find that Jovana was more put out than they were; she did not know what explanations to give Jovana or how to apologize for not having thought to warn her. As her fear subsided, she continued to tremble. Yolande listened to her replies, walking up and down with Aude waving frantically in her arms. Simone could not bear her look of relief; she felt suddenly swamped by her kindness and wished she would understand that they should leave.

I'm calling from Belgrade, Jovana explained, as though in desperate entreaty to them not to make her return home. Simone found it hard to discourage this irresponsible hope. The ceiling overhead creaked under Claude's footsteps. It had taken him all this time to force himself out of his nausea; those were the facts they had to obey. Simone explained to Jovana that he had barely gotten out of bed since the previous day, less to elicit sympathy than to convince herself again that they could not keep Gaël. Jovana replied that she understood and she would call back when she had her ticket.

Claude came down the stairs one at a time, as though his slippers would no longer stay on his feet. Simone told him that Gaël had been picked up at G. and Jovana was trying to find a flight for the next day—the tone of bitter irony she had noticed in Jovana's voice as she hung up gradually struck her as legitimate but terribly cruel. Claude nodded but did not try to protest; then he went to sit down in an armchair. Simone saw him take hold of the remote control and immediately put it down again. He sat bundled in his chair, clasping the armrests with both hands and staring out into the garden, where darkening shadows were sinking into the early evening warmth. His pain at having to let Jovana down for good was too much to watch.

He had not noticed that his son was there, or at least he had not said hello. Cédric reacted warily. He stared at him intensely, tapping his sweaty upper lip, more amused that annoyed to see Claude looking the other way, and probably intrigued, too, at the unrecognizable wide-eyed expression of dismay on his face. They must have had a real fight the other day, Simone realized, seeing Yolande put her hand over Cédric's in a gesture of restraint to forestall his anger (or his desire to smoke). The sleeping weight of Aude in her arms was becoming more and more unbalanced. Claude finally put on the television, and that was what persuaded them to leave. Cédric ran his hand through his hair, put his mobile phone away and announced, Right, we're going as he tucked his shirt into his pants.

Claude half-rose to say good-bye. His lazy left leg seemed to flex momentarily under his weight. Cédric gave a start, a shiver, when he noticed how weak Claude was. He must have thought that you can't get angry with a man in that condition, because he took a step forward and grasped his shoulder. Then, without waiting for anything in return, he turned to Yolande and took Aude from her, motioning to the door with his chin. Simone went out to the car with them. It was pleasant outside, with a slight breeze and a few last russet glimmers over the rooftops. It is an evening for taking a stroll, she thought with a pang. Cédric settled the child in the backseat and stood up to kiss her; Simone could not get over seeing tears in his eyes. His leg won't take his weight at all, he said in an oddly shocked voice. It's like he's suddenly gone downhill in two days. Simone did not know what to say in reply; she had too often thought in vain that the worst had come.

Simone had gone upstairs to freshen up when Gaël was brought back to them. She opened the skylight in the roof to overhear the brief exchange on the front step. Evening was falling, dark blue and curiously free of any hint of the riots; indeed, she did not even know if there had been any more. Two people had turned up, a man and a woman whose round accents seemed designed to allay the fathers' severity. Gaël mumbled a barely audible *Thank you*; then the footsteps and voices faded rapidly out to the car parked seemingly a long way off in the dark. Claude put the outdoor light on and gently closed the door. Simone heard him call Gaël into the study, where they stayed a brief ten minutes. He must have been insisting on his principles, although they would never restore good sense or peace as he hoped.

Simone slumped onto the edge of the bath, her arms resting limply on her thighs. The anguish of the day was morphing into a weariness from which she felt she would never recover. She was roused from her reverie by Gaël's sniveling protestations, followed by a great racket as he stomped, snuffling, up to his room. Simone stood up and paused for a moment to study her reflection in the mirror with the lucid, knowing intimacy that had helped her watch herself growing old. She was surprised to find the landing almost in darkness when she emerged. The air down the stairs was cooler now, and there was the gentle sound of sprinklers. Simone pressed her ear to Gaël's door. She thought she could hear him grumpily packing his bag, then jumping up and down on his bed, thumping on the wall. She knocked, waited a second, then opened the door a crack.

Gaël was leaning out the window; he swung around sharply, but his anger subsided when he saw her. He was arched against the wall, with the sill sticking into his back. A thin trickle of tears ran down from his puffy eyes. He must have been scared witless to have been lost for so long. Simone did not know how to apologize for their thoughtlessness. I was going to call you when I got there, but I got on the wrong train, he explained, as though inviting her to come in. Little bubbles of saliva glistened at the corners of his mouth. Simone wondered what he had eaten apart from the yogurt that morning. The street-lights had just come on outside and the leaves on the silver birch were lit up like snowflakes in front of the window. Gaël stood up, hearing the hiss of tires vanishing into the night. I didn't even know things had flared up again last night, he said, falling backward onto his heels. There was something sweet and almost reasonable about his despondency. He switched the bedside light on and off, and, for the space of an instant, Simone caught a glimpse of Claude in his expression. Your mother called a while ago. She's flying back very early tomorrow morning and she'll be here in the early afternoon. Simone saw him bravely register the disappointment of having so much time to wait. She put her hand out mechanically to take his knee, but her hand remained hanging over the edge of the mattress; she had nothing in reserve to cope with the time, either.

Claude had just come upstairs. It was dark on the landing and they heard him cough, then announce that he wasn't feeling well and wouldn't want any dinner. His voice was toneless, his strength depleted or gone. Gaël hardly seemed bothered. Anyway, I don't have to love him, he said in a final rush of bravado when Claude had gone into his room. Simone smiled at him, trying to dispel his sulky mood, and suggested they go and buy kebabs at the gas station. Contrary to expectation, Gaël made an effort to cheer up. He flung himself on his belly on the bed to grab one of the clean T-shirts already stowed in the bag. Simone was amazed to see him change in front of her, and she noticed a faint scar all the way across his chest, extending between his ribs. My lungs were all shriveled when I was born, he explained in answer to her surprise. He hugged himself, faking the pain he had presumably felt.

Simone drew her hands together on her lap; she was unprepared for the thought of Jovana at twenty having to deal with the agony of seeing her son subjected to such a serious operation while still a baby.

Gaël had preceded her into the garage, but he stopped pursing his lips in confusion, arrested by the smell. The window was down and smears from Claude's efforts to wipe up the mess on either side of the car door were drying out. Simone apologized and suggested they go on foot instead, but Gaël was not put off by the idea of helping to clean up. Simone went to fetch a bucket and found him some outsize gloves, in which he clumsily but conscientiously set about sponging off the door. This silent activity gradually restored his affectionate mood.

Everything was in darkness now beyond the open door, where a cloud of insects was hovering. Simone felt exposed, as though in a bubble. The sound of footsteps racing down the street made her hurriedly turn out the light. Suddenly, the darkness was lit up; the silhouette of the houses opposite appeared, and soon three shadows hurtled wildly past, taking long, angry young strides. Gaël shrank back behind the car. He agreed with Simone that they had better not go out. Their cheerlessness was perfectly matched. Simone had only just realized that she probably wouldn't see him again after he left the next day.

GAËL WAS AWAKE and ready, although it was not yet eight o'clock. Simone found him waiting for her in the gray gloom of lowered blinds. She was only just emerging from her first apprehensions on waking. Being caught with bare legs before she had showered and seeing him hanging around so early with nothing to do antagonized her. Yet she hadn't the heart to tell him to go back up to his room for a while; guilt shackled her with far too many misgivings.

He didn't know what he was hungry for, then wanted to fix his own slice of bread and butter, which he chewed with a long stare, swinging his legs under the table. Jovana had not called before leaving Belgrade. He was smoldering with resentment like a jealous lover. Simone was finding it increasingly hard to put up with his laziness about finding things to do on his own. She had spent the night with Claude, not daring or not knowing how to leave him in peace after that day. She felt she had slept only in short bursts of strange dreams. Her skin was prickling with tension and fatigue. She told herself that it was time for the little boy to leave now.

Huge patterned sheets with pale flowers were swinging all down one side of the garden. Malika kept appearing and disappearing, clearly intrigued by what was going on next door. Simone suggested Gaël invite her over to play with him. The idea drew a sigh from him; he thought he didn't know her well enough, but he finally went to join her at the fence anyway. Simone could see him giving laconic answers while he unwrapped the long tendrils of white bindweed from the metal mesh. The boredom of waiting was undermining even his usual instinctive affection for other people. Claude had still not gotten up, and it occurred to her to get out the Ping-Pong table that had languished for years in the depths of the garage.

She was just pushing aside some cardboard boxes when she noticed splintered glass in the back window of the car. The door was damaged, too, with a knee-level dent several centimeters deep. She froze in bewilderment and anger that Claude had said nothing about an act of violent vandalism. Gaël had followed her and was waiting to be told what to do in a corner of the garage. His reluctance was frustrating her, flaying her, wearing her down with a barely repressed urge to scream.

They set up the table in its old place under the plum trees, now considerably broader and thicker than a few years ago. Simone went back into the garage to find the paddles and calmly examined the damage done to the car. The door had buckled at the point of impact, with a hole of flaking paint where a stone had been hurled at full force. Claude had gotten up and was looking for her in the garden, but she didn't answer immediately. She needed to fill her mind with the calm, resolute thoughts that had been forming since the previous day.

Gaël had wandered off to watch Claude and was swinging around the pole of the rotary clothesline. Simone sensed that he was not so much resentful as self-conscious about making peace. She put the paddles down on the table and went to join Claude, brushing the dust from her clothes and preparing herself calmly for his criticisms about all the fuss. He was flexing his left hand, which edema had wrapped in a thick-feeling but apparently painless glove. Simone noticed coolly that he had taken a shower and put on clean clothes for Jovana. He had eaten nothing at all the day before. Gaunt and tired, he had a masklike stare on his completely hairless face. He must have seen his dead reflection in the mirror, she could not help thinking when he raised his eyes to her. What on earth could the people who assaulted the car have thought when they saw him like that? There was something utterly tragic about ending up so exposed to the world.

Gaël was dribbling the ball across the table, discreetly trying to attract attention. The heat was already intense and was drenching the fine curls of hair on the back of his neck. When he had hit the ball into the bushes for the tenth time, he asked Claude if he wanted a game with him. The suggestion made him blush, and Claude seemed not to know how to take it, or how to disappoint this affected effort at reconciliation. He tried to return a few balls, which he did awkwardly because he no longer had a good hand to hold the paddle properly. The strain and movement gradually turned the tense smile on his white lips into a rictus. Gaël stopped playing abruptly when he saw that Claude was going to be sick. He turned to Simone with a look of horror, as though to say *Sorry.* When Claude had left the lawn, stiff and bowed, transparent, Gaël went over to her, wiping his chin on the hem of his T-shirt. He wanted to know how long his father was going to be sick like that. Simone said a few days, thinking that it would more likely be a week. Tiredness was harassing her like a desire to flee. She gave herself a shake and went to pick up the paddle Claude had thrown into the grass. The green tabletop was covered in little sticky spots; she was irked to find that they were aphid droppings that had fallen from the plum trees. She thought she had heard the phone, and Gaël had already rushed to take it. She soon saw him come running back to tell her that his mother would be there in an hour. Simone guessed from his troubled face that he had only just realized they would not see one another again.

Jovana finally turned up not long after she had called. She must have heard a noise in the garden, because she appeared under the silver birch, dressed in a kind of aviator's plastic jacket, which was odd in such fine weather. Gaël flung himself at her and buried his face in her belly. She laughed at him and pummeled his head with her fist by way of scolding him for his nonsense. Simone guessed that she was really stifling a much more serious disappointment and displeasure. Claude had not come downstairs, and Jovana looked about for him as she came over to say hello to Simone, with Gaël tucked under her arm like a bag. She wiped her forehead on her sleeve before offering her cheek, apologizing again for the hassle. She seemed to Simone to have lost some of her spontaneity, and though Simone could not bring herself to say so, she thought that maybe they ought to offer to pay for her ticket.

Claude slowly emerged from the depths of

the living room, his face washed, his body ravaged under his ironed clothes. Jovana gave an involuntary start when she saw that he had changed yet again. He stopped a short distance away from them, with Gaël's bag at his feet and his hands on his hips. Simone realized that he must be unsure how he looked and smelled and that he had given up all desire to have a moment alone with Jovana. Anyway, it was clear that she had nothing more to give just for the sake of pointless, dispiriting memories. It was nearly midday, and she let Gaël go, explaining that she had come with a friend who was waiting in the car. Claude bent down to pick up the bag and led the way out to the street.

Jovana's friend was leaning against the trunk of the SUV, smoking a cigarette. He was a young guy of slight build, taut and slender, with thick light brown hair pulled back in a tight knot. He stubbed out his cigarette when he caught sight of Gaël running toward him and greeted him with short playful punches that made him blush with suspect pride. Claude was now at their side. He greeted the young man by holding out the bag in his waxen hand. Jovana made the introductions. The incongruity of the situation blurred her manners with cheerful, comradely bluntness. Simone hung back and watched them from under the birch tree, not wanting to confuse Claude, or Gaël, either, whose unrecognizable behavior already excluded them. Claude's emaciated body among them looked spectral. He doesn't even sweat anymore, thought Simone, steadying herself against the wall. The net curtains billowed out through the open windows of the study. She glanced up at the backdrop to her days for the past ten years, at the furniture that had never been hers. I won't stay a day longer than I have to, she promised herself, decisive and serene.

Jovana was coming over to her, taking springy steps enforced by her thick sneakers. He's changed again, she said, disconcerted and chewing at her full red lips. She had dark-green-and-gray eyes, just like Gaël's, and that fine youthful skin, prettily swollen in the heat. She's his soft, downy side, mused Simone in a surge of affection that was a bit out of place. We haven't been much help to you, she chimed in, trying to make light of it. Jovana shrugged her shoulders in reply, betraying more annoyance than she intended; indeed, her eyes clouded with smoky anger, which she dispelled by ruffling her bangs. Gaël had stretched out on the backseat and was watching them, propped on his elbows, while Claude waited stoically on the street in the pitiless sun. Jovana shouted to them that she was coming and moved to kiss Simone, giving off a surprisingly strong waft of perspiration. Her expression seemed to harden as she drew back. I love Gaël more than anything in the world and I'm not sorry about anything, she said, but you haven't the faintest idea how hard it was. Simone put her hand up to her throat and took a step back to take in the full impact of the rebuke. Everything in her recoiled at the idea of having to shoulder the guilt. You think it's because of me that Claude stopped showing up, she protested, emphasizing her words. Jovana looked as dumbfounded as Simone had been stunned, and a bit suspicious. Obviously, that was how she had understood things, and revising her opinion that day must have been hard for her. I said that so that you'd know, she conceded, her eyes on Claude, who was still standing motionless by the garden gate. Simone told her to get going; anyway, there were so many things that death would leave unresolved. Jovana made her promise hastily (thoughtlessly) not to say anything to Claude. Gaël had stuck his head and arm out of the window and was waving wearily at them. Simone realized that they had not even kissed good-bye and that, just now, she was not even sorry about it.

The Ping-Pong table was still out in the garden, and also a plastic chair, it, too, now sticky with aphid droppings. Simone had spent the day alone under the trees, in a peace she was cautiously rediscovering. As evening fell, Claude came down to join her. He felt less nauseated and had even managed to swallow a few crackers. The heat had not abated much. Simone went to open the windows upstairs and in the kitchen to get the air circulating now that the rain of rustling sprinklers in the neighboring gardens had revived it. Claude made a move to take her hand when she came to sit beside him on the sofa. His new, bald features smoothed out his expression. Simone was amazed he had not even tried to find out about the riots. She was suddenly aware that an irreversible gulf had opened up between them, between him and the world.

What happened to the car? she asked. Claude slowly turned to face her, as though she were accusing him. He aimed the remote control to change the channel and took his time to carefully word his reply. He had turned down a street cordoned off by the police and had not been quick enough getting out. The stone struck just as I was turning, he explained with odd reluctance. Did you manage to see who it was? Again, the question seemed to offend him, weary him. What makes you think it was aimed at me? Simone realized how pointed and insulting her questions were. But she had to know because she was going to outlive him—to know, too, why he had thrown Nora's stepson out of the club.

Claude slowly drew his hand over his face to wipe away a kind of sneer of disillusionment. The moron spat on two girls and their parents complained. The third time, I had to expel him. Anyway, he hardly ever came to the training sessions. He's a dealer, if you must know, but of course nobody notices anything. It was said in the tone he had used at the time of the trial, the voice of his worst conflicts and disappointments, which he had been so keen to die from. Simone apologized and took his hand, but he gently withdrew it with a twitch of pain. She was hungry but dared not talk of food. Noises from the street reached them through the open windows. They heard two scooters pass by, then a man talking loudly on the phone. A light breeze was picking up, and the Ping-Pong ball, which had been left out on the table with the paddles, rolled off into the grass. Claude was starting to fall into a doze, his chest rising to the rhythm of the weak rattle from his diseased lungs.

Yolande called late that evening. On the verge of tears, she told them that Cédric had been traumatized to see Claude so reduced and to have argued with him in his condition. Simone could find nothing sincere to think or say that might have comforted them. She had had a long talk with her brother earlier in the evening. He suggested she spend a month with them when everything was over, and that was what she aspired to now: peace and freedom from responsibility.